Ride the Jericho Road

Twenty-year-old Thad Forrester considered himself and expert at the fast draw without ever having fought a gunfight. Then, after his parents were murdered in cold blood, Thad vowed revenge and along with his friends, Coop and Rowdy, he set out on what seemed a thrilling adventure.

However, revenge must take second place in their scheme when the trio pledge to rescue a kidnapped child from the outlaw enclave of Jericho. Whilst Rowdy plans to spirit the young girl away from the refuge, Thad finds his parents' ruthless killer is also walking the streets of Jericho.

Against overwhelming odds, can these inexperienced young men hope to win the inevitable showdown?

Ride the Jericho Road

Wade VanMarten

A Black Horse Western

ROBERT HALE · LONDON

© Wade VanMarten 2005
First published in Great Britain 2005

ISBN 0 7090 7781 5

Robert Hale Limited
Clerkenwell House
Clerkenwell Green
London EC1R 0HT

Typeset by
Derek Doyle & Associates, Shaw Heath.
Printed and bound in Great Britain by
Antony Rowe Limited, Wiltshire

CHAPTER 1

'You ready for this, Thad?' Rowdy asked, sweat dripping off his nose.

'Old friend, I'm ready as I'll ever be,' Thad answered.

'But there's two of 'em,' Rowdy reminded him.

'I know, I know,' Thad replied. 'Now get out of the way.'

Thad Forrester stood with his feet slightly apart, the left slightly ahead of the right one. His gun hand was at his side and he wiggled his fingers to keep them loose and relaxed.

Rowdy stepped back and nodded to Coop. 'Let 'em go and run!'

Coop turned and ran.

Thad drew his .45 and fired twice then thrust the pistol back into its holster. His targets lay on the ground in pieces. The strings that had suspended the whiskey bottles hung loose, moving slightly in the faint, hot breeze that blew from the south.

'Wooee!' Rowdy hollered. 'That's the best shootin' I've seen yet! Thad, danged if we shouldn't call you Deadeye Dick. You're ready to go up against Jesse James, Johnny Ringo and Wes Hardin all at once.'

They had hung the whiskey bottles from two branches of the tallest mesquite tree they could find. Coop pulled them to the side and released them about a second apart so they were swinging separately. Thad drew, fired twice from the hip and shattered both bottles.

Thad Forrester and Rowdy Mason both were twenty. Coop Carter was nineteen. The three loved to ride, shoot, make noise and hold off growing up as long as possible. They shot at tin cans and bottles, and like young boys, pretended that they were shooting desperados.

They had grown up shooting. They tried all kinds of shooting: careful, deliberate marksmanship, shooting from the hip and shooting from horseback. They all agreed that shooting from horseback was the stuff of campfire tales, not practical marksmanship.

In the informal shooting contests Thad came out on top. He carried a Colt Double Action 1878 Frontier .45 with a five and a half inch barrel that allowed him to draw, fire and return the weapon to its holster almost faster than the eye could follow.

Rowdy Mason carried a Colt .44 Henry rimfire and Coop carried an old Calvary Model Colt .45 with a seven and a half inch barrel. Both referred to their single-action weapons as 'old thumb-busters'. While both lacked the convenience of Thad's newer double-action model, they acquitted themselves well in the accuracy category.

The three friends had for years come to 'their shootin' range' outside Apache Wells, Texas, a small, busy community west of Pecos in sight of the Apache Mountains. The 'range' was between two hills and was far enough away from the main road that no one gave them any trouble over their noisy recreation. They had started as small boys when Thad's father had let them use an old smoothbore muzzleloader that had been in the family for decades. They had to buy their own powder and cast their own balls as a condition of use, but they loved it enough to spend hours scavenging and melting lead then pouring it in the molds. They bought powder from Haverkamp's gun shop with money carefully saved from doing chores.

Thad won, hands down, as best fast-draw-fire-from-the-hip marksman. He explained to his friends how he did it.

'When I reach for the gun, my finger goes on the trigger. I start squeezing right then so when the barrel clears the holster, I'm halfway through the trigger squeeze. The trick is to bring the pistol up on the target and finish squeezing the trigger so I've aimed at the same time the hammer falls. I dang near shot my own danged foot off trying to get the feel of that trigger. But when I got it, I knew I couldn't be beat. Now putting the pistol back in the holster as soon as I've fired is all for show. If I ever really shoot someone, I got to make sure he's dead or dying and that he's through shooting before I reholster my weapon.'

Thad did not recognize the bravado of those words being spoken by a young man who had never been in a gunfight.

Thad Forrester was the son of Cam and Mary Forrester. Cameron Forrester's law career had made him a legend in Apache Springs and surrounding Mescalero County. He was known as a fair, non-judgmental, efficient and compassionate lawman, something rare in Texas in the last half of the nineteenth century. Despite being brave to a fault, he had lived out several terms as county sheriff and retired in good health with only a few scars he kept covered up and never mentioned.

The locals knew Thad, Rowdy Mason and

Coop Carter jokingly as the three musketeers. Coop's mother was dead and he and his father were not on the closest of terms. Rowdy had been an orphan for years and was beholden to no one. About once a week, Mary Forrester invited her son's two friends over for supper, knowing neither had a mother to cook for them. Tonight was to be the night.

Thad was a slender six feet one weighting one hundred seventy five pounds. He had sandy hair, blue eyes and a ruddy complexion. His quick, clear and direct eyes were inherited, along with his straight nose, from his mother. His father's jaw, square and strong, finished out a face that the girls considered handsome. Of the horses that his father kept, the one he called his own was a buckskin named 'Cochise'.

Cooper Carter was shorter, about five ten, brown haired and brown eyes. He had lived among Latinos and had a decent command of the language spoken along the Texas-Mexico border. He was more bookish than his two friends but never mentioned it. He had several books in his possession that he read at night and on Sundays, one of which was a collection of Shakespeare's plays. The only outward manifestation of his penchant for literature was calling his jet black gelding 'Othello'. He was fond of discussing his friend's foibles and mistakes with

Othello, leaning over and talking into his ear, loudly enough for them to hear of course.

Rowlett 'Rowdy' Mason had been an orphan as far back as he could remember. He grew up in an orphan asylum, fighting for every scrap of food he got. He grew up faster than his contemporaries and eventually earned respect as a fighter. He could break a nose, gouge an eye or rip a cheek with the best of them. He left the orphanage at age twelve and started earning his own living doing odd jobs and working cattle. By age eighteen, he was six feet, three inches tall and weighed two hundred twenty-five pounds., His face, featuring a crooked nose acquired in a street fight and dark eyes that matched his hair was a bit too lumpy to be called handsome. However, his face wore a stamp of amiability that led men, women and especially children to like and trust him. He ended up in Apache Wells hiding from El Paso lawmen who claimed he had beaten a local tough within an inch of his life. He wore a white hat and rode a dapple-grey gelding he called 'Traveller'.

After Thad's stunt of shooting two swinging targets from the hip, the boys decided to call it a day and mounted up for the ride back to town. As they rode, Thad brought up a subject they usually avoided.

'My folks are pressuring me to get a regular

job, fellows. Looks like I'm going to have to give up those temporary jobs we've been working like riding fence, and rounding up strays and branding and stuff. My dad said he didn't raise me to be a saddle bum or trick shot artist.'

Rowdy laughed and said, 'Sometimes it's nice not having any folks to give you a hard time. I reckon I'll get me a job when the time comes.'

Coop asked with a chuckle, 'How do you know when the time has come, Rowdy?'

Rowdy squinted one eye and did some mental calculating. 'When I fancy a girl real bad and she keeps slappin' my hands off her and I figure I got to have her, I reckon I'll finally have to marry up and start supportin' a family. That'll be the time.'

'I was wondering when one is going to let you get that close,' Thad said with a guffaw.

'You're bein' a smart Alec again,' Rowdy pouted.

Coop spoke up. 'Oh gosh, Thad. Didn't you know that old Rowdy has been sparking Leona Threadgill. I hear she kind of likes him, all two hundred fifty pounds of her.'

'What do you mean, two hundred fifty pounds?' Thad said in disbelief. 'She'd *dress out* at two seventy-five!'

'Oh heck!' Rowdy groaned.

'Lands sakes, Rowdy,' Thad said. 'There's an awful lot to love there and it's just waiting for you.

Besides, you'll never be cold on a winter's night. She'd just snuggle up on you and wooeee!'

Thad and Coop cackled.

Rowdy, tiring of the ribbing, spurred Traveller and cried out, 'Last one to the Cactus Flower buys the beer!'

The three disappeared in a cloud of dust.

That night, the boys ate all they could hold of Mary Forrester's beef stew, fried okra, corn on the cob, turnip greens and apple pie. When they finished, they leaned back in their chairs holding their stomachs and groaning.

'Miz Forrester, ma'am,' Rowdy said. 'That was the best chuck I ever ate in my whole life.'

Mary Forrester laughed her deep-throated laugh and said, 'Rowdy, that's exactly what you say every time you eat here.

Coop said, 'She's right, Rowdy. You're going to have to say something new or she's going to think you're just talking to hear your head echo.'

'Well, shoot!' Rowdy exclaimed. 'It's true. Ever since I eat here, it *is* the best I ever ate cause it gets better every time.'

When the laughter around the table died down, Cam Forrester said, 'Boys. Thad's been telling me you have been talking about getting steady jobs.'

Coop's and Rowdy's faces took on sombre miens.

'Yes sir, we *have* been talking,' Coop said. 'But so far that's all we've done. There's just not a lot around here for young fellows like us to get started on.'

'I'll tell you what I told Thad,' the father said, lighting his pipe. 'Don't shoot for the moon right off. Try some things, see how they feel. Then, when you decide you want to try to make one your life's work, learn everything about it you can. Try to anticipate what's needed, don't wait for somebody to tell you.'

'That's good advice,' Coop said. 'I reckon we could learn about a little something 'sides cattle work before we jump in for good.'

'The thought of it kinda scares me,' Rowdy said. 'But I reckon I gotta bite the bullet sometime.'

'That's the spirit,' the older man said. 'You've got a whole life ahead of you. Just don't screw it up!'

The conversation went on for another hour while Thad's mother cleared the table and washed the dishes. Much to Thad's relief, she didn't ask him to do his usual chore of drying the dishes while his friends were guests so he could take part in the 'main talk' between the young men and Cam Forrester.

Forrester knew the boys were fond of the many tales of bank robbery, rustlers, swindlers and bad men in general. When he related a story, he always managed to find a small nugget of wisdom in it, a subtle moral that he hoped his audience would remember. Since he was the closest thing to a father that either had, he felt it was his duty to train them as well as he did his own son.

Finally the hour was growing late and the two guests stood up to go. They kissed Mrs Forrester on her cheeks and thanked her profusely for the excellent meal, found their hats and rode off into the night heading for the room they rented from a widow lady on the other side of town.

Thad waved goodnight and watched them ride away. His father stood beside him on the front porch and watched the boys leave.

'I'm sorry that your mother and I didn't have more children. It would have been nice for you to have a little brother or a big brother to learn from. But we didn't so you'll have to make do with those two.'

'They are good friends, Dad,' Thad said. 'We'd stand up for each other no matter what.'

'That's good, Thad. You can never tell when you'll need a friend to stand beside you.'

As Thad listened to those words, he had no idea of how prophetic they were.

CHAPTER 2

Two days later, Thad climbed out of bed and pulled on his jeans and boots. He looked at his face in the mirror and decided he had better shave since he was going to talk to Mr Norris down at the general store about going to work there. He glanced out the window of his room that looked out over the road and was surprised to see his dad standing by the front gate talking earnestly to Sheriff Wells. He went about his shaving and careful dressing then went downstairs.

He was eating breakfast when his father walked in wearing a serious expression.

'What's going on, Dad,' Thad asked. 'Was that Sheriff Wells you were talking to?'

Cam Forrester smiled and said, 'Yes, it was. There was just some routine stuff he wanted to ask me about, an old-time crook that used to hang around these parts.'

'From the expressions on your faces, he must be hanging around here again,' Thad ventured, prompted by his curiosity.

'I hope not,' Forrester answered, laughing. 'Fortunately, no one has seen hide nor hair of that rascal. Mary, you have any more coffee?'

Knowing that his father did not want to discuss it further, Thad dropped the subject.

The interview with Mr Norris went very well. The store owner was impressed with Thad's ability to add long columns of numbers and to divide and multiply. He spoke favourably of a training program for Thad. The training program would allow Thad to learn the duties of his position at no charge while he worked without a salary or wages for some indeterminate period. At the end of it, Thad would be taken on full time or let go, depending on his performance. Norris told Thad he would make a decision by the next day and to come back tomorrow.

Thad walked away from the store feeling good about himself and the fact that he had taken the first step toward independence.

He walked toward Hiram Flowers' Legal Office across the street. He thought he might as well look in on Lila Beth. She clerked for her father, the only attorney in town, and knew everyone's business. However, her father knew she was the soul of discretion and took her responsibilities to heart.

Thad pushed the door open and walked into the outer office. Lila looked up anticipating one of her father's clients and her face broke into a wide smile when she saw Thad. But then she remembered that she was impatient with him and the smile disappeared.

Lila Flowers was considered the most desirable young lady in Apache Wells. She was eighteen years old with dark chestnut hair that hung to the middle of her back; dark brown eyes and a figure that caught young men's eyes and made old men think sinful thoughts.

'Well Thaddeus,' she said in a businesslike tone, 'what can we do for you today?'

Thad smiled, looking impish. He knew he looked like a naughty little boy when he smiled and he knew females couldn't stay angry with him when he did.

'I couldn't very well come to town and not come by to see you,' he said, trying his best to look sincere. 'You know I can't let a day go by without seeing your face or hearing your voice.'

Lila harrumphed. 'Don't pull that little boy charm on me,' she said sharply. 'You must not have wanted to go riding and shooting or you wouldn't have time for me.' Her voice took on heavy sarcasm. 'Wasn't it just yesterday that you and your friends came riding into town, whooping and hollering like wild Indians, scaring the children and kicking up dust. I suppose we should be thankful you three weren't firing your pistols into the air like drunken trail hands.'

Thad looked hurt and Lila felt her resolve slip a little.

'If you want to know the truth,' he said, 'I've been talking to Mr Norris over to the general store about a job.'

'A job doing something that doesn't involve riding horses and driving cattle! I don't believe it!' she said, her blue eyes wide in feigned astonishment. 'A clerk in a store. I thought you'd at least become a Texas Ranger or a deputy sheriff or something like that. They won't let you shoot your gun up and down the aisles of the general store, you know.'

'All right!' he said, throwing up his hands. 'I give up. I was going to take you to lunch over at Miz Daurene's but I reckon I'll just forget it.'

'Oh no you won't,' Lila spat.

She jumped up from her desk, opened the door to her father's office and said in her sweetest little girl tone, 'Daddy, could I go to lunch a little early. Thad wants to take me over to Miz Daurene's.'

Thad heard Mr Flowers answer, 'Why sure. Go ahead honey.'

Lila blew her daddy a kiss and closed the door, smiling. She put on her bonnet, took Thad's arm and hustled him out of the law office toward Miz Daurene's.

'Let me tell you right now, Thaddeus Forrester,' she said. 'I'm not going to wait forever for you to become capable of supporting a family. I'm eighteen years old already and I have no intention of being an old maid.'

To make her point, when a young cowboy passed by and tipped his hat, she smiled broadly. The gesture did not go unnoticed. Thad knew full well that Lila Flowers was just about the prettiest girl in the county and could have her pick of the single young men. He found himself feeling slightly uncomfortable.

During their meal at Miz Daurene's, Lila chattered on without let up about a wide variety of subjects including two of her friends who had already married, one well, the other not so well. She even chattered about the mess down in the capitol at Austin though Thad exhibited no interest in politics and never had. She talked about Dick and Anne Cartwright and the fact that Dick Cartwright drank so much, Anna made him sleep in the barn most of the time. Finally she stopped talking and Thad thought she had run out of breath.

She was silent for a while then looked up at

Thad and spoke in a low voice. 'Do you really care for me, Thad?'

Surprised by the question, Thad answered,' Of course Lila. You know I do. There has never been anyone else but you for me. Why do you ask?'

'You've told me how much you want me and that you'd die if you didn't have me.'

Thad glanced around to make certain no one could overhear. 'Yes, that's true,' he whispered. 'But this isn't the place to be talking about that.'

'What I want to know is how long can you wait to marry me? It all depends on you getting into a responsible line of work and making a living. If we get married and have a child, I won't be able to work and help pay expenses; you'll have to carry that on your own.'

Thad sat for a while, thinking, his brow furrowed and biting his lower lip. Then he said, 'Lila, I reckon I'd wait for however long it took. I just want to make sure we *do* get married before I have to walk down the aisle leaning on a cane and using an ear trumpet.'

Lila laughed at the vision of Thad with an ear trumpet but tears came to her eyes and she quickly wiped them away.

'One more year. Let's wait one more year,' she said. 'By then, you'll know if you can make a living and I should be able to get my father to pay me some kind of salary for the work I've been doing for nothing. By then, maybe we can see our way clear to getting married.'

Thad, challenged by the first real plan in his life, hesitated then said, 'That's it then. We'll work and save up something and see how things are. But things will have to be pretty bad for me *not* to marry you.'

Lila reached across and squeezed his hand. 'Oh Thad, just think! Only one year and maybe, not even that long.'

At supper that evening, Thad told his parents about the plans he and Lila had made. He cautioned them that everything had to be right for him to take the final step. He said he didn't want to live with Lila Beth in a hand to mouth situation.

Mary Forrester said, 'If you are made of the same stuff your father is, you'll find a way.' Then she smiled a big knowing smile at her husband.

The Forrester home was built on several acres that Cam had bought on the edge of town. It faced the Stevenson place on the other side of the main road. There were several sheds in back of the house, along with a barn where the Forrester horses were kept. After supper, Thad was in the barn pitching some hay down from the loft when he heard a gunshot. In a few seconds, there was a second one. Alarmed, Thad shinnied down the ladder and ran outside in time to see a man on horseback galloping away down the main road.

'Dad!' he called and started running to the house. He ran in the back door through the empty kitchen calling, 'Mom, Dad' and getting no reply. When he ran into the main hallway he saw them. The front door was standing open and they both lay in front of it. His mother was motionless but his dad was crawling on his stomach, reaching for her and calling her name.

'Oh God!' Thad cried when he saw the blood.

Cameron Forrester put his arms around Mary and tried to get a response from her but none came. He kept repeating, 'Mary, Mary, talk to me!'

Thad fell to his knees beside his parents. His father's shirt was soaked with blood and more was pouring out.

'Dad! what happened? Who did this?' he cried, weeping uncontrollably.

His father turned his face to him and gasped, 'Isaac Cripps . . . Jericho.' He then turned back to Mary's pale face and stroked her cheek. His head fell on her breast and he lay still.

Thad was calling to his dead parents when John Stevenson from across the road ran in the front door. 'I heard shots . . .' He stopped in mid-sentence. He went back through the open door and called to his son, 'John Junior, get your horse and get into town. Bring back the doctor and the sheriff! Hurry!'

CHAPTER 3

The funeral for Cameron and Mary Forrester
was the biggest that the town had ever seen.
They had known and were known and liked by
practically everyone in the county. There wasn't
much business conducted that afternoon, most
of the shops and offices downtown were closed
for the services. Even the Cactus Flower Saloon
closed for two hours. Some of the mourners
were still in shock, shaking their heads over the
suddenness of it. The minister said words of
praise for both the deceased and everyone knew
the words were true.

Rowdy and Coop sat on the front row with
Thad. Lila sat beside him holding his arm, weeping when he wept. She had loved he Forresters
too, having known them since her childhood.

Back at the Forresters' home, Lila helped with
the food and the cleaning up then her father
took her home. After the mourners had gone,

the dishes were cleaned up and the house was still, Rowdy and Coop remained. They hadn't talked with Thad very much. They didn't know how to console a friend in the face of such a tragedy and words came with difficulty. They knew the shock was wearing off and he was terribly quiet and brooding, something they had not seen before.

There was a rap at the door and Thad got up and answered it. It was Sheriff Wells.

'May I come in and talk for a few minutes?' he asked.

'Sure,' Thad said and led him into the parlour.

The sheriff greeted Rowdy and Coop then sat down.

'I just wanted to tell you what I know about the man that shot your parents, Thad,' he said.

'I'd like to know,' Thad said.

The sheriff leaned forward in his chair and said, 'You know that a man named Isaac Cripps killed your parents. What you don't know is why. That reason is that almost sixteen years ago, your father arrested Isaac Cripps and got a conviction. Cripps has been in the state penitentiary for fifteen years. He was released about a week ago after serving his term.'

Thad spoke up. 'That was what you and my dad were talking about that day out here in front of the house.'

'That's right,' Wells answered. 'The state people notified me Cripps had been released. A couple of weeks before he was released, a John Burgoyne, another ex-convict and an old riding partner, visited him. I came out here to tell your dad and the reason I did, was that when Cripps was sentenced and was being led away he promised he would come back and "get even". Now Cripps never cared one way or another for what people thought of him, but the way your dad took him into custody humiliated him.'

'What was that?' Thad asked. His two friends leaned closer, intent on the sheriff's words.

'Isaac Cripps and four of his friends held up the bank downtown. They got the money and started out but Cam Forrester was waiting outside for them when they came out. Cam shot down two of them right there. Those two never made it to their horses. Cripps and the other two got mounted up and were shooting at everything in sight. They started riding but Cam was in the street shooting at them. He emptied one six shooter and pulled out another one. He shot Cripps' horse right out from under him. Cripps spilled into the dirt, dropping the money he was carrying and ended up on foot. He ran into a little shop that back then was close to the bank. Cam emptied his pistol at the two galloping out of town and hit one and made him drop his money bag but he kept going.'

Cam ran into the shop after Cripps. Cripps grabbed a lady that was in the shop and put his gun to her head and told Cam to back off or he'd kill her. This particular lady was one of the sweetest, best and most pious ladies you'll ever hope to see and Cam had known her for years. Cam backed off and Cripps told him to put his gun down. Cam did and Cripps pulled the gun off the lady's head and aimed directly at Cam. But when he pulled the trigger, his weapon was empty! I am told that when that hammer clicked, the expression on Cripps' face was a joy to behold. Cripps threw down the pistol and pulled a hunting knife out of his belt and tried to cut the lady's throat. But Cam grabbed his arm, got that lady away from Cripps, fought Cripps for the knife and took it away from him and beat the living hell out of him right there. He threw Cripps out in the street and beat him up some more. By the time they carried that so and so to the gaol, he wasn't even recognizable.

'Cripps hated Cam for the beating. I think he'd rather that Cam had killed him rather than humiliate him that way. When they led him away to state prison in chains, he was wild-eyed, slobbering and raving about getting even with Cam. Then he had fifteen years in that hell hole to brood on it and let it fester.'

The sheriff leaned back and said, 'That's the story. It's too bad that Cripps didn't get the noose for that bank job but no one got killed, at least not in that one. It's a wonder, because Cripps is one of those people that have no conscience. Human life means no more to him than a cockroach does to you or me. He needs to be let off this earth and the sooner the better.'

'What about Burgoyne?' Thad asked.

The sheriff said, 'He's just as bad as Cripps if not worse. I understand he held up a church one time during Sunday night services and stole the collection money while the service was going on. When the minister, who was a small man, tried to stop him, Burgoyne didn't bother to knock him down which he could have done with one hand. He just pulled his pistol and shot him right there in the church.'

'Good grief!' Thad said.

'And before he left, he shot the sexton who was just trying to get out of the way.'

Thad asked the sheriff, 'What did my father mean when he said, "Jericho"?'

Wells said, 'He was referring to that Godforsaken place south of here where Cripps used to hide when he wasn't robbing and killing. It isn't exactly a town though I understand there are buildings and businesses. But no one lives there that's not an outlaw, a fugitive of some

28

kind or a social cripple. There's no law except the six-gun. The meanest and quickest on the trigger runs the place. There's not a lawman in Texas, and that includes the Rangers, that will set foot in the place with less than a dozen heavily armed men behind him.'

Rowdy asked, 'Why don't the state send an army of men down there and clean it out?'

Wells nodded. 'They've considered it. They figure before they got within miles of the place, the outlaws would run and get across the border into Mexico. No one figures it's worth the risk.'

'Do you think that's where Cripps headed after he left here?' Thad asked.

'That would be my guess,' Wells answered. 'Besides, there's been a story around for a long time now that Cripps stashed the loot from a big job somewhere around Jericho before Cam Forrester sent him to prison. If that's so, he'll head straight for it because he'll need some money to put together a gang.'

'How much loot?' Coop asked.

'No one knows,' Wells responded with a chuckle. 'Some stories have it in gold, others in cash. But the most likely truth is that it's only a story. I personally think the story is an invention to get people to do things for him.'

Wells got to his feet. 'I just wanted you to know about Cripps, son,' Wells said to Thad. 'I figure you need to know the whole story.'

'Thanks for coming by, Sheriff,' Thad said. 'I appreciate it. I had never heard of Cripps until my dad spoke his name.'

The sheriff tipped his hat and went out the door.

As the sheriff rode away, Thad turned to his friends and said, 'I'm going to Jericho and I'm going to kill Isaac Cripps.'

Rowdy and Coop sat stunned, staring at Thad in disbelief.

'Have you gone completely loco?' Coop asked. 'That's a one-way ride if I ever heard it!'

Rowdy spoke up. 'If you don't get killed on the way down there, those outlaws will roast you alive! That's crazy talk, Thad.'

'Fellows,' Thad said. 'I have been thinking about this. Nothing has ever hurt me like losing my parents. And losing them the way I lost them makes me so angry I can't even describe it to you. The last thing my dad said to me was the name "Isaac Cripps" and "Jericho". I feel like he wanted me to do something. Why else would he say "Jericho" unless he wanted me to go there?'

Coop, always the level-headed of the three, said, 'Thad, your dad was dying. He was looking at the woman he cared about more than anything in the world lying there dead. I think you are putting words in his mouth because it's an emotional time. I don't think your dad would want you to risk your life to "get even" with Cripps. Why don't you think about it for a while longer? Think about Lila Beth too. What is she going to say? If you get yourself killed, it's not only your life you'll be missing out on; it will be Lila too.'

'Somethin' else to think about, Thad,' Rowdy offered. 'It won't be whiskey bottles you'll be shooting at. It will be real men, bad men with tied-down holsters. And from what the sheriff says, the worst of 'em all is the one you're after.'

'Think about it a little longer,' Coop said, almost pleading. 'Will you at least do that?'

Thad sat with his head down, looking at the floor. 'I'll think about it one more night, fellows, then I will make my final decision. If I have decided to go by tomorrow morning, I'm going down to see Mr Flowers and make out a will. After that, there's no turning back because this thing is eating my insides like a damned lobo is chewing on 'em.'

Coop and Rowdy made a detour on their way home from Thad's house. They stopped by the Flowers' house to talk to Lila. They explained to her what Thad was planning and asked her to use her considerable powers of persuasion to change Thad's mind. Then they went home, leaving Lila to toss and turn in her bed most of the night.

The next morning, both of them were at Miz Daurene's drinking coffee when Thad rode into sight. He went straight to Flowers' law office and tied up in front. They saw him hesitate at the door, take a deep breath and go in. They looked at one another and Coop said, 'Well, I suppose that is that.'

Rowdy answered, 'I reckon so.'

Thad walked into the law office and Lila looked up at him with red-rimmed eyes.

'We've got to talk,' she said.

Thad smiled grimly. 'I see that Coop and Rowdy wasted no time in running and tattling, did they?'

'Can we talk?' she asked.

'After I talk to your dad.'

She looked like a thundercloud but went to her father's office door and rapped. When he answered, she said, 'Thad Forrester is here to see you.'

'Send him in, Lila. I needed to talk to him anyway,' Flowers replied.

Thad went in and closed the door. In a half hour, Hiram Flowers came out and told Lila to go next door to the saddle shop and find two people to be witnesses. Lila got two local cowhands to come to the office. They watched Thad sign his will then signed their own names as witnesses.

When his business was finished, Thad spoke to Lila. 'You want to talk now?'

'It appears that it is too late for me to talk,' she replied. 'You are going off to get yourself killed, aren't you?'

Thad ignored the question. 'My dad and mother left everything, the homestead the animals and the land to me. I just made out my will dividing all of it up between you and Coop and Rowdy. You'll get half, they'll get half between 'em.'

The tears started to flow. 'I don't want your property, Thad. I want you. Please don't do this thing. I'm afraid, terribly afraid you won't come back.'

Thad's expression hardened. 'If I don't do this thing, I'll shrivel up inside and I might as well die. I could never be happy again, even with you, without making things even with Cripps. I'd go to my grave knowing that my parents died before they could ever see their own grandchildren because that . . . a worthless piece of trash killed them and I did nothing about it. I'm sorry Lila. If I don't come back, just remember that the last thing I thought of was you. I'll be thinking of you every minute, seeing you in my mind waiting for me and that will keep me going.'

He turned to go. 'Now I've got a lot to do before I leave. I got to get busy.'

'When are you leaving,' Lila asked with a sigh of resignation.

'Tomorrow at first light,' he replied. 'Can I come by tonight to say goodbye?'

'I don't think that's a good idea, Thad,' she answered.

She looked down and he saw tears falling. He turned and walked out. After he mounted his horse and started up the street, he saw Rowdy and Coop standing in front of Miz Daurene's place. They stood quietly, nodding to him as he rode by.

The next morning just as the sky in the east started to lighten, Thad walked out of his back-door with his bedroll and tied it down over his saddlebags. He returned to the door and locked it then paused to take a look around. He had arranged with John Junior from across the road to see about the stock and take care of things while he was gone so he knew the place would be in good hands. He made a last minute check. His spare clothes were in his bedroll, along with two canteens of water for himself and a canvas bag of water. There was also a bag of oats for Cochise when they camped on the trail. His Winchester Model 1866 Henry .44 carbine was in the saddle holster. He had trail food, ammunition and his father's spyglass in his saddlebags.

He mounted up and nudged Cochise into a trot and rounded the house. When he saw who was waiting for him in front, he reined to a stop and stared in wonder.

Rowdy and Coop were both mounted up and carrying gear much like his own. Lila sat beside them in her father's buckboard.

'What do you two think you are doing?' he asked.

'Well,' Coop said, 'You don't think we were going to let you go on a big adventure all by yourself do you? Why, you would come back and tell all these stories and we wouldn't know whether they were true or not. There's no way we were going to let you do that then come back. We figured we just go along so we'd have some stories too.'

'You know you are welcome,' Thad said. 'But danged if I wasn't looking forward to a few days on the trail without listening to you two tell lies and bad jokes.'

The two boys chuckled then looked at Lila. She stepped down from the buckboard and walked up to Thad's horse.

'If I was a man, I'd go with you,' she said. 'But I'm not, so I can't. I just came to say goodbye. This way we'll keep it short.'

Thad dismounted and took her in his arms. 'My God, I love you!' he said, his voice catching

35

in his throat. He kissed her on the mouth, tasting the sweetness of her and feeling her soft body in his arms and doubts flooded over him. He fought those feelings because he knew there was no turning back, no matter how much he ached for her or how frightened he was of the task he had set for himself.

'I love you,' she whispered when the kiss ended. 'Please come back.'

'I will, I swear,' he said.

He released her and climbed back into the saddle. Looking at his friends, he nodded and clicked his tongue, urging his horse into motion. Coop and Rowdy fell in beside him and they headed south.

Lila stood on the buckboard watching them in the light of the rising sun until they were out of sight.

CHAPTER 4

'Thad, do you even know what this Cripps fellow looks like?' Coop asked.

Thad gave him an impatient look. 'Why of course. I got a full description from Sheriff Wells. Did you think I was just going to ride south until someone pointed him out?'

'Just asking,' Coop said. 'What *does* he look like?'

Thad recited the description from memory, 'Five feet, ten inches tall, one hundred and sixty-five pounds, hair dark brown turning grey, brown eyes, knife wound scar over left eye about two inches long. Nose has been broken and has a lump going to the right. For relaxation he likes to hurt females. Spends time in whorehouses, sometimes mistreats the whores.'

'Sounds like a nice fellow,' Coop observed. 'You wouldn't expect him to be passing the plate down at the Baptist Church would you?'

Thad added, 'John Burgoyne is just about the same kind of person. You remember that the sheriff told us about my dad shooting one of the bank robbers but he stayed on his horse?'

'Yeh, sure, we remember that,' Rowdy said.

'They believe that was John Burgoyne. When someone arrested him later on for some other thing, he had a bullet scar in his left side where a bullet had gone through and cracked a couple of ribs.'

'What does *he* look like?' Coop asked.

'Big, about six two, two hundred fifty pounds, strong as an ox. Sandy hair, receding off his forehead, blue eyes, one of them clouded over some, square jaw, broad nose, has several knife scars on his arms. Head's too big to wear most hats. Wears a blue bandana around his head or something like it.'

Coop leaned over and told Othello, 'Boy, if we see that pilgrim, head in another direction.'

'That fellow sounds like he might be a little hard to handle,' Rowdy said. 'You aren't planning to wrestle those birds at any time are you?'

'Nope,' Thad said, chuckling. 'That pilgrim I'm going to shoot from a distance. Or maybe one of you are going to shoot him.'

'If it's all the same to you, I'll shoot him while riding by at a full gallop,' Rowdy said.

That evening, they bought water from a Mexican goat herder who called himself Carlos. Carlos lived with his wife and two children in a little adobe with a sweet water well right beside it. They camped by an old tumbledown shack about a mile past Carlos' place. They made coffee and made supper of tinned meat and biscuits.

Coop was the only one of the three who spoke Spanish or at least a Mex-Tex version of it. He negotiated with Carlos for the water and afterward seemed to chat on about something.

Rowdy, his curiosity aroused, finally asked, 'What was that you and Carlos were talkin' about Coop?'

Coop explained, 'I was waiting until we were by ourselves to tell you about that so we wouldn't get the old fellow too excited. I asked him if, in the last few days, two men came through, one with a broken nose and a scar over his eye and the other with a rag wrapped around his head. He said that they had come by and demanded water. He also said he was scared half to death because the scarred one had the look of a crazy person from his eyes. He did not argue with them about the water because he was afraid for his family.'

'Holy smoke!' Thad said. 'Good judgement.'

'I told him that we were looking for those men

and that they were very bad,' Coop added. 'He wished us "Vaya con Dios".'

'I got a feeling we're goin' to need the Almighty's help,' Rowdy said.

'Don't worry Rowdy,' Thad said. 'You heard the preacher at the funeral. God is on *our* side.'

'Even though we are going to try to kill somebody?' Rowdy asked.

'Sure,' Coop said. 'We are on the side of the angels.'

There were three towns they would pass through before they got to Jericho. They were Cruz, the closest, then Yucca, Amargosa and finally Jericho. They planned to spend the night in Cruz. It was late in the day when Cruz came into sight. They rode into the town down the only visible street and found what passed for a livery stable. They made arrangements to put up and feed their horses and asked the stable keeper where they could get something to eat and a place to stay.

The stable keeper said that they could eat at the cantina down the street. It was the only place that served food ready to eat. As for sleeping accommodations, he said, 'My heart is broken to tell you there are no beds for rent in this town.'

'Where can we put up?' Thad asked.

'You can pitch your bedrolls in the hay in the

loft for twenty-five cents each,' the man said, smiling apologetically. 'But,' he added, 'there is no smoking allowed.'

The boys made the arrangements and headed for the cantina. They found the menu limited to beans, rice and enchiladas and the music limited to Mexican tunes that none of them recognized. The young Latina who waited on them was slightly amused by the three and flirted playfully. She said they could have cheese enchiladas or meat enchiladas.

'What kind of meat is in the meat enchiladas?' Coop asked.

The girl looked unconcerned and shrugged her shoulders at the question.

Thad said, 'That means it could be cow, horse, dog, rabbit, armadillo or whatever was unlucky enough to wander through. I'll have the cheese.'

The other two ordered the same thing and they washed down the fiery mixture with *cerveza.*

When the waitress came to collect for their meal, the young men told her to keep the change. Since the change amounted to a generous tip, she became even more demonstrative. She was attractive in a tawny, wild animal kind of way that appealed to Coop and he started flirting with her in earnest. After she brought more beers, she playfully sat in Coop's lap and caressed his cheek.

The beer relaxed the three friends and they were enjoying Coop's flirting with the girl. Suddenly, there came a roar and a huge Anglo strode to the table and grabbed the waitress by the arm, jerking her out of Coop's lap.

'You gonna learn to behave yourself, you little slut!' he roared, shoving her across the room. Then he turned to Coop and roared in the same manner, 'Keep your hands offa my woman, you little son-of-a-bitch.'

'I didn't see a sign around her neck with your name on it, big boy,' Coop said lightly.

The big man was dumbfounded by the smaller man's lack of fear in the face of danger. He roared and lunged for Coop.

There was a flash of steel and a click as Thad drew faster than anyone could see and poked the pistol's barrel into the big man's face.

'Hold it, fat mouth!' Thad shouted.

The big man froze where he was, staring down the bore of Thad's .44. Thad was on his feet holding the pistol unwaveringly six inches from the man's nose. All eyes were on the angry man's face and no one noticed Rowdy getting out of his chair.

'Now, we are going to walk out of here,' Thad said. 'Since this big fellow spoiled the evening for us,' he announced, 'we're going home and go to bed.'

Coop almost burst out laughing at that.

Coop got up and he and Thad backed towards the door. As they neared the door, Thad lowered the pistol and shoved it back in its holster. With a roar, the big man started for Thad and Coop. He had taken only one step when Rowdy grabbed his arm, spun him around and hit the man a terrific blow on his nose with his fist. The big man went down and rolled back and forth moaning and holding his nose.

The three friends made their escape from the cantina and walked back to the stable, laughing as they reviewed the incident.

Coop crowed, 'That great big fellow who was big enough to win the war all by himself gave up and surrendered after getting one little nose broke.'

'The great booby never knew what hit him,' Thad said. 'First off, there's a pistol in his face, then we start out funning him then Rowdy breaks his nose. I loved it!'

Rowdy chimed in. 'I was going to punch him in the chin and knock him out but then I got a close look at that chin and it looked like an anvil! Heck, I wasn't goin' to punch an anvil with my knuckles, that's why I went for his nose. Sure did crunch! Did ya hear it?'

The three reached the stable and sat down. They were still congratulating themselves when a

Latino walked in wearing a white Stetson and a marshal's badge. He stopped and observed them carefully without speaking. The three stopped chuckling and looked at the lawman.

'Is there something we can help you with?' Thad asked.

'Yes, there is,' the marshal said. 'I am Marshal Esau Morales. I came to see the brave people who embarrassed Moose Broussard back at the cantina.'

'You are looking at them,' Thad responded. 'And we didn't start that fracas if you're looking for someone to blame it on.'

'I know, I know,' the marshal said quickly. 'As usual, Broussard started it. But this time you finished it. His nose is a mess,' he added, looking at Rowdy.

The marshal's movements and attitude did not indicate hostility or tension. The boys began to relax.

'Who are you boys and where are you from?' the marshal asked.

Thad said, 'I'm Thad Forrester, the big fellow with the fists there is Rowdy Mason and that one over there is Coop Carter. We're from Apache Wells.'

'Apache Wells, huh,' the marshal grunted. 'What are you doing all the way to Cruz, Texas where nothing happens and no one gets rich?'

'We're just passing through, Marshal,' Thad said. 'We are on our way to Amargosa.'

'Amargosa? Why would three well-fed Anglos want to go to Amargosa?'

'I have a cousin living there,' Thad said. 'We are going for a visit.'

'You usually take your holidays on a battle-field?' Morales asked, narrowing his eyes.

'Uh, what do you mean?' Coop asked.

The marshal looked at Coop in surprise. 'You mean you don't know about the war going on there? It's a land war. It's the newcomers against the old homesteaders. The last man standing up without a bullet hole in him wins.'

The boys looked at one another blankly.

'Now,' the marshal said. 'Why don't you quit the bull shit and answer this one question. What the hell are you boys up to?'

Thad had been sitting on a workbench. He stood up and said, 'I'm going to Jericho to kill Isaac Cripps.'

For a moment the marshal was struck dumb. He recovered his voice and said, 'Cripps? *Es de los que el Diablo empeno y no volvio por ellos.** Why are you on this fool's errand?'

Thad responded in even tones, 'Because the son-of-a-bitch killed my mother and father.'

*One so bad that even the devil disowned him.

45

The marshal looked embarrassed. 'Cripps just got out of prison,' he said, his brow wrinkling. 'When did this happen?'

'Five days ago,' Thad replied.

'These men are your friends?' Morales asked, tilting his head toward Rowdy and Coop.

'Yes,' Thad replied.

The marshal took off his hat and sat down on a packing box. 'Since I cannot stop you, I will give you this advice. You are young men. You have your lives in front of you. Go home, go back to Apache Wells and get drunk and chase girls and have fun. Despite what you did back there in the cantina, your hide cannot turn bullets. Don't throw your lives away in Jericho. Let God deal with Cripps.'

'What if God doesn't want to deal with Cripps? Should he do for us what we are too afraid to do ourselves?' Thad asked. 'No. I can't turn back now. This thing must be done. These men are here because they chose to come with me on their own. They are free to return any time.'

The marshal looked at Rowdy then at Coop with raised eyebrows. 'You choose to stay with your friend?'

Both nodded.

'Since you are determined to do this thing, let me tell you what I know of Cripps,' the marshal said.

'Please do,' Thad replied.

The marshal found a box and turned it over so he could sit on it. He sat down and looked at his feet for a few moments then started to speak.

'The strongest and worst memory I have in my whole life is of Isaac Cripps.' The marshal crossed himself and went on. 'It was here in Cruz. I was with a friend my own age, nine years old. His name was Jesus. I was visiting him at his parents' house and we were playing some game, running around barefooted and half naked because our parents could not afford to buy shoes or clothes for us. They had two other children, younger than we; a boy and a girl. Jesus and I were in a back room when his mother came in and said to Jesus, "One of your father's associates has come to visit him. You boys go outside!" We went but we didn't go far. Jesus was curious as to what this mysterious man wanted with his father so we crept back to a window and listened. The two men were arguing. I knew from his accent that the visitor was an Anglo. The more they argued, the louder the voices got. I became frightened because Jesus' father was supposed to have obtained something from a messenger but apparently had not and the Anglo accused him of stealing it for himself. I could not understand what the thing was but it must have been very valuable. The Anglo's language became horribly obscene and I had never heard of such things. I turned to Jesus and told him I was going home for a little while and I would come back later. I ran home and told my mother that Jesus' father had a big problem with an Anglo. She told me to mind my own business.'

Marshal Morales took off his hat, pulled a handkerchief from his pocket and wiped his face and forehead. He put his hat back on and continued.

'I stayed at home for a while, perhaps an hour and a half. Being that young, I had no real concept of time. Then I went back to Jesus' house. There was no one outside so I went to the door and knocked. No one came. I pushed the door open and called Jesus. There was no answer. I could not understand where they had all gone. I went into the house and I saw Jesus' father lying on the floor covered with blood. I saw a foot sticking out of a doorway and went to see who it was. It was my friend Jesus. His throat had been cut and his head nearly separated from his body. I was in what you would call a trance. I felt that all of it was a horrible dream and I would wake up in a moment. I went into the bedroom and saw Jesus' mother on the bed. Her breasts . . . never mind the details, but that man had done horrible things to her. There was a movement in the corner of my eye and I looked up into the face of Isaac Cripps! I was raised to be afraid of Satan, but fear of Satan was nothing compared to what I felt that day. I must have run from the house screaming, I do not remember. They told me I was out of my mind for three days. Of course, they found the bodies and thought that seeing such horrors damaged my mind and I would be an imbecile from that day onwards. Others had seen Cripps enter the house and told the sheriff. The sheriff questioned me but I could not utter a word. I was in that condition for weeks. Eventually, they left me alone and my voice came back very slowly. I was fifteen years old before I could bring myself to speak of that day. I learned later that he killed all of them, the children too, with his knife. The thing that stands out in my mind is that Jesus' mother did not die a quick death.'

The marshal bowed his head for a while then stood up, put on his hat and said, 'That is what I wanted to tell you.'

The boys were silent, stunned at the story the marshal had told.

'Thank you Marshal,' Thad finally replied. 'We know more of what we are up against now. If we are still alive in a week, we will come back through and say hello.'

The marshal turned and looked at Thad. 'You

will not be alive in a week. Your bones will bleach on the sands after the worms have picked them clean. If you come back to Cruz in a week, do not stop to say hello, because you will be ghosts. Please do not stop in Cruz. We do not need the trouble. Pass us by. *Vaya con Dios!*'

He turned and walked out.

'How about that!' Coop exclaimed. 'We have just been disinvited by Cruz, Texas.'

'From what I've seen fellows, it's a small loss,' Thad said.

'We must not look like much,' Rowdy said. 'Everyone we talk to calculates that we are going to be killed.'

'Maybe they are judging us by themselves,' Coop said. 'After all, none of them has seen fit to go after Cripps. Are they going to wait until he comes back and robs their bank and cuts up some of their citizens?'

'Let 'em hide their faces,' Thad said with disgust. 'We'll do what they should have done a long time ago. Now, let's get some sleep. We have a long day tomorrow.'

Rowdy said, 'After hearing that story, I just hope I *can* sleep.'

CHAPTER 5

Despite the minimal accommodations, the trio slept well in their bedrolls on the hay. The next morning, Thad went to the marshal's office and obtained a crude, hand-drawn map of the road to Jericho. It had notations as to the location of fresh water, the towns on their route and an estimate of the miles from place to place. This done, they followed their noses to the back door of the tavern where a substantial Mexican lady had made coffee and was cooking tortillas. They breakfasted on the corn treats, goat butter and coffee then continued on their way.

As they travelled south, the terrain grew dryer and seemingly more hostile. The sun was merciless and they slowed their pace to conserve the horses' stamina. They ate their midday meal by the side of the road and continued onward. The sun was setting when they reached the next town, Yucca. Again, they found there were no accommodations for travellers and they would have to pitch their bedrolls in the stable behind the blacksmith's forge. They made arrangements for the horses to be fed and watered then walked to a small café a few doors down the main street. As they supped on roasted goat and discussed their trip, Rowdy mentioned Cripps. At the word, a cowboy who was sitting close by turned and looked sharply at them, unnoticed except by Thad. He hurried through his meal and left, glancing back at them as he went out the door.

After their meal, the trio stood on the board-walk in front of the café and surveyed the street. There was little activity and the only noticeable sounds were coming from a saloon several doors away.

'Think we should look at the saloon before we go to bed?' Coop asked.

Thad gave him a rueful look. 'I don't think that's a good idea. The last time we went into a saloon, your little romance got us in trouble.'

Coop laughed. 'They wasn't exactly a romance,' he said, chuckling. 'It was more of a quick feel and pinch.'

As the three laughed, Thad noticed a scruffy-looking person across the street wearing a derby hat, a toothpick in his mouth and leaning against a post. Thad looked to his right and saw another idler perhaps forty feet away.

'We have company,' he said softly.

From their left, a tall, rough-looking man dressed in rumpled, nondescript clothing and a greasy cowman's hat approached them. He stopped ten feet away and looked at them with a pronounced sneer on his face. He was incredibly ugly. His eyebrows had grown together in a single wavy line that reminded the observer of a hairy bird in flight. His teeth jutted in odd directions from a scarred mouth like a botched jack-o'-lantern. He wore a large pistol on his hip.

'Are you the nancy boys that have been talkin' about my friend, Isaac Cripps?' he asked, smiling grotesquely.

Thad stepped in front of his friends and whispered, 'Watch the other two. I'll take care of this one.'

Coop and Rowdy took positions facing the two idlers who were watching the proceedings intently.

'What's it to you?' Thad asked. 'What we talk about is none of your concern.'

The bizarre smile abruptly disappeared from the questioner's face. 'My friend Cripps is gonna be the new boss of Jericho. I ain't gonna let some little turd like you mess him up. Who do you think you are anyway?' he rasped.

Coop saw the post-leaner across the street straighten up and spit the toothpick out of his mouth. Rowdy watched the other observer twitch uncomfortably and wipe at the sweat on his face.

'I *know* who I am,' Thad said. 'I actually knew my father. How about you?'

The ugly man roared with rage and reached for his pistol. It had cleared the holster when Thad's shot hit him in the chest, knocking him backwards. The grotesque man looked surprised and tried to aim. Thad fired again and this time his antagonist's knees buckled and he sprawled face down on the boardwalk.

The man across the street started to draw but Coop outdrew him and yelled, 'Don't!'

The man left it in the holster and put his hand to his side.

When Thad had fired his first shot, the man opposite Rowdy had turned and run into the darkness.

Thad returned his pistol to its holster and walked to the man bleeding on the boardwalk. He felt for a pulse in his victim's neck and finding none, stood up and said with a slight quiver in his voice, 'Let's go back to the barn fellows.'

Just before they reached the stable, Thad ran off the path, bent over and vomited.

His two friends watched him for a moment then Rowdy said, 'I gotta go to the outhouse,' and sprinted to the back of the stable.

Coop looked at his hands as if they belonged to someone else. They were shaking violently.

When Thad stopped vomiting, he walked into the stable and Coop followed him. They sat down on two boxes and soon were joined by Rowdy. A single kerosene lantern lighted the interior of the stable for a few feet.

'So now we know how it feels to kill someone,' Coop said.

Thad looked at him and said, 'Sorry about that, fellows.'

Rowdy looked chagrined. 'My bowels turned to water! Cold water!'

'We had to learn sometime,' Thad said. 'You think about it a million times but when it happens, it's different.'

'That was clever, Thad, calling that man a bastard to his face,' Coop said.

Thad nodded. 'I wanted him to draw on my timing, not his own. I thought goading him might make him mad and throw him off his pace.'

'I'd say it worked,' Coop said. 'It's a good thing for us his friends didn't amount to much. That might have turned out badly.'

Rowdy chuckled. 'For us, yeah. As it was, it didn't turn out too good for that ugly jehu.'

'Don't speak ill of the dead,' Coop said then laughed.

When Coop laughed, Thad and Rowdy started laughing almost uncontrollably. All three laughed till tears of relief rolled out of their eyes.

When they finally stopped and caught their breath, Coop said, 'I feel better.'

The other two agreed.

'Hope you boys are having a good time,' came a voice from the doorway.

They turned to see a man wearing a badge holding a six-shooter on them. A footstep behind them told them that another gunman had them covered as well.

The lawman walked into the stable and said, 'I'm Marshal Maggs. You three are under arrest. Get your hands up.'

'Under arrest for what?' Thad asked, raising his hands.

'For the murder of one of our leading citizens,' Maggs answered.

'If that was one of your leading citizens, this town is in deep shit,' Thad retorted.

Maggs growled and backhanded Thad in the face. Thad made no sound but glared at the marshal.

'Get their weapons!' Maggs ordered.

The man behind them pulled the pistols from their holsters.

The marshal waved his pistol toward the door. 'Let's get over to the gaol. Move it!'

The five men walked into the street with Maggs and his deputy holding pistols on their three captives. They moved up the street to the wonder of a few passers by until they reached the gaol. The deputy opened the door and the trio walked in.

'Search 'em,' the marshal ordered.

The deputy went through their pockets removing everything, pocket knives, wallets, money, coins and handkerchiefs. He put it in a pile on the marshal's desk along with their pistols. The marshal unlocked a cabinet standing against a wall and put their pistols in it and relocked it using one of about twenty keys on a metal loop he took from the wall.

'Put 'em in separate cells,' the marshal ordered and the three were ushered into the rear of the building where a small lantern illuminated three cells. The deputy shoved the three into the three cells and the marshal locked the door of each.

'What's this all about, Marshal,' Thad asked. 'That man challenged us and started to draw. It was a fair fight.'

'That's not what the witnesses will say, young fellow,' Maggs said, grinning. 'After you get a fair trial and are hanged, your property, money, horses, saddles and weapons will be confiscated and used to defray the cost of your trial. But don't worry, you'll get a decent burial at town expense.'

He went out and closed the door.

'Is this really happening?' Coop asked.

'Unless it's some kind of strange joke, I think it is,' Thad answered.

The door opened and Maggs said, 'You have a visitor.'

A plump little man, impeccably dressed in an expensive suit with a satin waistcoat and with several gold rings on his pink, plump fingers walked in. The deputy brought in a chair and put it down behind the plump man who gingerly sat down and crossed his legs at the ankles.

'I am Nero Adams,' he said. 'I own this town and you have created a disturbance. More than that actually, you murdered one of my most trusted employees, Skeet Eldritch.'

'Bullshit!' Thad yelled, making the plump man jump. 'He drew on me. It was a fair fight.'

Adams recovered his composure and smiled. 'The marshal assured me that you would make that plea. Fortunately, we have some solid citizens that say otherwise.'

'What do you want?' Thad asked. 'You come in here just to bend our ears and gloat?'

'I just wanted a look at you. You see, since two days ago we have had an arrangement with an old friend, Isaac Cripps, to give him certain assurances and perform certain services.'

'And those are?' Thad asked.

Adams giggled. 'Those are to interfere with the plans of anyone who seeks Mr Cripps. When one of Mr Eldritch's associates overheard you three discussing Mr Cripps, he notified Mr Eldritch, as you can see, with disastrous results. But Mr Eldritch's grieving family will have the satisfaction of knowing his murderer received his just punishment.'

'What do the relatives of a pile of shit look like?' Rowdy asked sarcastically.

Adams ignored him.

'Wait a minute,' Coop said. 'Cripps just served fifteen years in prison. Where does he get the money to bribe a whole town?'

Adams smiled. 'Mr Cripps has some, ah, investments in which we have confidence. We are happy to perform our services "on credit" so to speak.'

Adams got to his feet and turned towards the door. 'Ta, ta, young gentlemen. The next time I see you will be at your hanging. I assure you your passing will not go unnoticed. We plan to make it a festive occasion.'

With that, he went out the door and the marshal closed it behind him.

In a few minutes, the marshal came back in and said, 'I'm going home and get a good night's sleep, fellows. Deputy Claunch will be spending the night in the office just in case. If you've got to pee, use the buckets under your bunks. If you have to take a dump, call Claunch. He'll escort you to the privy out back. Good night gentlemen.'

With that he left.

'You reckon they are really going to hang us, Thad?' Coop asked.

Thad answered, 'If they aren't, they're doing a pretty good job of bull-shitting us, aren't they?'

Thad looked at Rowdy who was fiddling with something in his hands.

'What are you doing, Rowdy?' he asked.

Rowdy held his right index finger to his lips. He held up a furry shapeless thing so that Thad and Coop could see it. In a moment, he reached back into a tear in the thin mattress on his bunk and pulled out some more horsehair. He busied himself twisting and pulling for several more minutes while the other two watched. Finally he held up his handiwork. It was a black, hairy spider of intimidating proportions, or at least, a very good imitation.

They waited, sometimes pacing, sometimes dozing until they estimated that the time was about three o'clock in the morning. Then Rowdy stood up and called out to the deputy.

'Deputy Claunch, Deputy Claunch! I got to go

and I got to go right now.'

There was a stirring from the office and the door opened.

Claunch stuck his head through and asked, 'What's the matter?'

'I got to go, Deputy. All this stuff has upset my shitter and I got to go,' came the answer.

'Hell, won't it wait till morning?' the deputy asked, rubbing his eyes.

'No!' Rowdy cried. 'It's goin' to come out and I cain't hold it. I'm gonna shit all over this floor!'

'Aw hell,' the deputy exclaimed. He pushed the door open and came into the cell area, jingling the keys on the big key ring.

'Step back against the wall!' he ordered Rowdy.

When Rowdy stepped back, Claunch unlocked the door, pulled out his pistol and waved Rowdy out. Rowdy came out dancing, taking hurried fast little steps and moaning.

The deputy directed Rowdy to the back door and out of it to the privy in back. Thad and Coop looked at each other and listened. They heard the voices of Rowdy and the deputy in low tones and they heard a door close. In a moment, they heard someone cry out then the deputy shouted. After that, there was silence until they heard a dragging sound.

Rowdy walked in through the back door dragging Deputy Claunch who appeared to be totally unconscious. He dragged the deputy into the vacant cell and locked the door with one of the keys on the big key ring.

Rowdy looked at his friends. 'Deputy Claunch here is terrible afraid of spiders. That one I found inside the privy just plumb scared him half to death when I tossed it at him.'

Thad could hardly keep himself from shouting out loud as Rowdy unlocked his cell door. Rowdy quickly unlocked Coop's cell and the three went into the office and lit a lantern. With the keys they unlocked the gun cabinet and retrieved their firearms, pulled open the desk drawer and took back their personal effects but could not find their money.

'That son-of-a-bitch marshal probably just stuck it in his pocket,' Coop spat.

They searched farther and found a metal lock box in a bottom drawer. In moments they had smashed it open and found a quantity of paper money.

'The jackpot, fellows,' Thad exclaimed.

Coop stuffed the money into his pockets and they went to the door. After cautiously peeping out, they swarmed out, closed the door and locked it then headed for the stable. When they passed a watering trough, Rowdy dropped the ring of keys into the water.

They filed into the barn noiselessly and located their horses and saddles. They were delighted that Maggs had not yet had time to confiscate them and move them elsewhere. They filled their canteens and water bags, saddled their mounts, and rode quietly out of the stable and down the main street to the south side of town.

'Goodbye Yucca,' Thad said, and they spurred their horses to a gallop.

CHAPTER 6

Their emergency provisions were still in their saddlebags and they had oats for their horses so they wasted no time in putting distance between themselves and Yucca. The stretch from Yucca to Amargosa was a considerable one and would require them to camp on the road.

The sun was three quarters of its way across a cloudless sky when they saw something on the road in the distance. As they got closer, they could see that it was three mounted men coming toward them. Finally, as the two groups came together, Thad saw that the other travellers were a disreputable lot. Their shirts were encrusted with salt and their hats were greasy with age. Their saddles were worn and cracked in places, testifying to continued neglect of the leather. The leader was a hard-looking man who had not shaved in several days. His eyes were dark brown and deep set and hard. He wore two single-action, nickel-plated Colts.

One of his companions looked at Thad's saddle and mount hungrily with light grey eyes. His eyes were the unfocused kind, the kind that when someone looked him in the eyes, his own seemed to focus behind that person. The other companion looked feebleminded and did not talk.

'Well, where you boys headed?' the leader asked.

'We are on our way to Amargosa,' Thad said. 'Going to do a little visiting.'

'Watch you step while you're there,' the leader said. 'There's a lot of gunplay going on.'

'Oh,' Thad said. 'Why's that?'

'There's some folks fightin' over land. The Mexes say that the big boss Nick Beale is stealin' land and killing Chicanos and all kinds of stuff,' the man answered. 'Soon's you ride into town, they want to know whose side you're on. If you give 'em the wrong answer, they may let daylight into your liver on the spot.'

'Sounds like a rough place,' Thad said looking at Coop and Rowdy. 'We'll watch our step. Where are you heading?' Thad asked.

'We're on our way to Cruz and maybe on north,' came the answer.

'When you pass through Yucca, better watch your step,' Thad said. 'The law there is sort of unreliable.'

'Oh, well, we'll remember that, won't we boys?'

The two companions smiled and nodded.

'It's a far piece all the way to Amargosa,' the two-gunned man said. 'You plannin' to make it today?'

'No, I don't think so,' Thad answered. 'We'll have to camp after a while.'

'There's good water about ten mile ahead,' two-gun said. 'It's a good place to camp.'

'Thanks,' Thad answered. 'We're much obliged to you.'

Two-gun spurred his horse and said, 'Adios.'

'Good bye,' Thad said.

The two groups rode on.

'I didn't like their looks,' Coop said as they rode on.

'I didn't either,' Rowdy said. 'That funny-eyed one looked at my horse and my gear like he'd like to have it.'

'Mine too,' Coop said.

'There were two things I didn't like about those worthies,' Thad said. 'First, the leader wore two guns. Only gunfighters wear two guns or lawmen that show off. I never heard of any decent lawman that wears two nickel-plated six-shooters. Second, all three of those pilgrims were wearing chaps. They were travelling cross-country and wearing chaps. When do you wear chaps, boys?'

Coop said, 'When I know I'm going to be riding in brush, like when we are working stock.'

Rowdy nodded. 'Who in the world wants to wear chaps when they are not riding in brush. The damned things are too hot.'

'Or maybe, Thad said, 'when you know you are going to be cutting cross-country to get away from a posse?'

The three were silent for a moment then Coop spoke, 'Who's going to sleep with one eye open tonight?'

Just before sundown, they found the camping spot, a patch of green in a wasteland. There was a spring that fed out cool, clear water into a pool where the horses drank. The riders filled their canteens and water bags and made coffee.

Rowdy sat by the small fire sipping his coffee and said, 'I'm glad them Yuccans didn't get around to confiscatin' my coffee pot. That would have been serious.'

'Almost as serious as hanging us, eh Rowdy?' Coop asked.

Thad was wandering around the campsite. It had been used countless times by various travellers some of whom had built lean-tos as shelter and some of them remained. Some were older and had lost their thatching and were merely frames. The lean-tos were built with the rears or closed ends toward the road so that someone approaching them from that direction could not see whether they were occupied or not.

He returned to the campfire deep in thought.

'Men,' he said. 'After our encounter today I think we should take some precautions.'

'I like them big words you use,' Rowdy said.

'What I propose,' Thad went on, 'is sleeping over there on the other side of the spring. It's plenty warm, so we don't need a fire next to us. We can leave our fire right here like we were sleeping in a couple of these lean-tos. If some-one takes a notion to jump us in the night, we'd have some warning.'

'Sounds good to me,' Coop said. 'I keep remembering that fellow's eyes.'

When Rowdy nodded his assent, they made the necessary moves. They moved their horses away from the approach to the road and laid out their bedrolls on the far side of the pool. They built up a campfire with a few branches they found, dried horse droppings and old cow flop. Then they turned in.

Thad figured from the stars that it was just past midnight when he heard a sound from the direction of the road. It seemed to be the sound of a horse's hoof on hard ground. He nudged his two companions awake. They lay in relative darkness looking across the spring at the low-burning campfire.

Suddenly there was the sound of galloping hoofs. Three riders going hell bent for leather were charging towards the campsite at full speed. As they reached the camp, they started firing into the lean-tos, two with pistols, the other with a rifle. They charged past the lean-tos firing into the little shelters point-blank, then turned and kept firing.

At that moment, Thad, Coop and Rowdy started firing at the mounted men. A horse fell, the rider screaming as he was pinned underneath. Thad shot one of them with his carbine and the man fell from his horse. The terrified horse charged into the night. One rider realized from where the ambush was coming and started firing wildly in the direction of the trio. Coop took careful aim in the dim light and fired. The man lurched backwards in the saddle and his panicked horse ran. As the horse swerved by a mesquite bush, the mortally wounded man fell out of the saddle onto the ground.

The firing stopped abruptly. There were no more targets for the boys from Apache Wells and there were no more assailants to fire back. Their first full-fledged gun battle was over and they were alive.

It was Coop's turn to know what it felt like to kill a man. He grew very silent.

At dawn, they inspected the bodies for identification and removed the gunbelts. What money the dead men carried, they took, put into a pouch and kept it separate. They rounded up the horses and checked them for injuries. Except for the dead one, the horses had escaped being hit. Coop and Rowdy threw ropes around the dead horse and using their own mounts, dragged it about a quarter mile downhill from the pool. They had no digging tools and the ground was rock hard so they carried the three bodies in the same direction they dragged the horse and buried them together under rocks.

Rowdy asked, 'Do you think we ought to say a few words over these fellows?'

'You think it will help, Rowdy?' Coop asked.

'I dunno,' Rowdy said, 'but it can't hurt and I'll feel better.'

They removed their hats and stood by the rock cairn they had stacked over the bodies.

Coop said, 'Lord, we don't know much about these fellows except they were no damned good. They were planning on shooting us in our beds, but we shot them first. Course, it's up to you as to what you do with their souls. We just arranged for you to have a little talk with them yourself. Amen.'

They got back to the camp and Coop stood on his toes to talk to Othello. He told the horse,

'Thad Forrester sure knows how to arrange exciting trips. I don't think I've been bored once.'

Thad grinned at Coop's ribbing and the trio, taking the outlaws' horses in tow, started once again for Amargosa

Amargosa was a larger town than the others they had visited. It actually boasted an hotel with a stable next door. The three wasted no time in checking into the hotel and arranging for a hot bath.

Rowdy finished his bath and said, 'Hooee! That was just in time. I was startin' to get crusty all over.'

The boys broke out their straight razors to take advantage of the hot water and shaved. Coop observed that Rowdy was not quite so scary after he scraped the hair off his face.

'Maybe now the dogs won't bark at you and little children won't run crying for their mamas,' he added.

After cleaning up and making a change of clothing, the trio went next door to a café for dinner. The waitress who took the order was singularly tall, almost six feet. She was a raw-boned girl with blond hair and blue eyes. She had strong features, almost manlike. But when she smiled, there was no doubt of her femininity. Thad noticed that when Rowdy ordered, she took particular interest.

'Rowdy,' Thad said as the girl walked away, 'I think that windmill-fixer likes you.'

'Huh?' Rowdy said. 'She does?'

'Sure, just keep an eye on her,' Thad assured him.

They were enjoying their sit-down meal when a short, olive-complexioned, square-built deputy sheriff walked in and came up to their table. He wore a pleasant countenance.

'Pardon me, gentlemen,' he said, smiling. 'Are you the party that just recently came into town leading two extra horses? And one of the horses had a gun belt holding two nickel-plated pistols looped over the saddle horn?'

'It might be us,' Thad said warily. 'Depends on who is asking and why.'

Coop and Rowdy dropped their forks and scooted their chairs back from the table to make drawing their weapons easier.

'Wait a minute, wait a minute men,' the deputy said hastily. 'I'm not looking to arrest anyone.'

'Let me tell you something, deputy,' Thad said. 'In the past couple of days we've been called out, arrested on trumped-up charges, threatened with hanging and ambushed in the middle of the night. We don't trust anybody including a nun from the holy Sisterhood because she might be packing iron under all those robes. Now state your business and don't beat around the damned bush.'

The deputy's words came out in a rush. 'You rode into town with two horses that belong or belonged to some bad people. What we want to know is if you are friends with those people or whether you killed those people and took their horses.'

Thad looked at his companions then said, 'The men that owned those horses tried to kill us last night and instead lost their own lives. Unfortunately, a stray bullet killed the third horse. The three men that rode them are buried out there in the desert not too far from a watering hole. Is there anything else you want to know?'

The deputy smiled broadly. 'Those men you killed were Buck Hawkins and his henchmen. He is, or was, the meanest son of a bitch who ever walked on two legs. His right hand man, Harry Fletcher, the one with grey eyes, was a monster who liked to do bad things to people. The third one was just a poor unfortunate creature who blindly did what he was told. If you have sent these creatures to their reward, you have done the world a great service.'

'That's good,' Thad replied, somewhat relieved. 'But there's something else. Since those animals are ours now, we're looking to sell 'em, the saddles that go with 'em and the firearms of their former owners. If you would put the word out, we'd appreciate it because we're running short of money. We got robbed by some guardian of the law in Yucca.'

The deputy smiled broadly. 'I'll do that, gentlemen. By the way, what are your names?'

'My name is Thad Forrester. This here's Rowdy Mason and Coop Carter.'

'Nice to meet you, gentlemen. My name's Roy Fresquez. I'll let you get back to you supper. So long.'

'It's nice to meet a law man that didn't try to shoot us or rob us,' Rowdy remarked, turning back to his meal.

'Yeah, but who is he going to talk to now?' Coop wondered out loud. 'And what is *that* person going to want?'

Thad nodded agreement.

The trio found out what the next person wanted of them when they returned to their hotel. A solid-looking, grey-haired gentleman was sitting in the small lobby when they walked in. He stood up and introduced himself as Hugo Aldama.

'I need to talk to you,' he said. 'Is there some place private we can go?'

'Sure,' Thad said. 'It will be a little crowded but we can talk in our room.'

The four of them climbed the stairs to room

11 and went in. Aldama sat on one of the two chairs. The boys made themselves comfortable on the beds.

'We have a very bad problem here in Amargosa. There is a company whose name we know only by rumour that seeks to acquire extensive land holdings in this area. We were not aware of this activity until the deaths of two landowners in the eastern part of the county. They were of Mexican heritage and their families had lived in this country for generations. A month apart, these two men sold their land to a holding company for cash, then were shot to death immediately afterward and robbed. The first one, a Pedro Nunez, we viewed as a terrible coincidence. The second one, Jesus Fernandez, made us realize that it was robbery on a sophisticated level. Since the second death, they have changed their tactics. They have started a campaign of intimidation against the landholders. Fences have been cut, stock has been scattered or stolen. Working horses have been shot, barns and homes have been torched. After the damage, the owner is confronted by a representative of the company with an offer to buy his land at a fraction of what it's worth.'

Aldama paused to collect his thoughts and Thad asked, 'My first question is what is the law doing about this.'

Aldama shook his head. 'Nothing that we can tell. The sheriff keeps making excuses, not enough men, no eyewitnesses, no solid evidence . . . in other words, he's putting us off.'

'Is this his usual operating method?'

'Good heavens no,' Aldama answered. 'Sheriff Rogers has always been completely dedicated to his job, honest to a fault, speaks fluent Spanish, married to a Mexican woman. As good a man as you could ask for in that job. And before you ask about the Rangers, we have sent letters and telegrams to the State Attorney General. We have received no acknowledgement of our efforts. We believe that our messages are being intercepted and never reach their destination.'

'Have you tried going to Austin to speak to the authorities there?' Coop asked.

'Yes. My close friend Alfred Nunez left two weeks ago to do just that. We have heard nothing. His wife is almost hysterical.'

'What is it about the land that makes it so important?' Thad asked the older gentleman.

'Rumours of great wealth,' he replied. 'Nothing specific. But it seems that someone believes something of value is under the earth, perhaps gold, perhaps precious stones, who knows?'

Coop looked at Thad. 'Apache gold,' he said.

Thad nodded in reply.

'What's that?' Aldama asked.

Coop explained. 'For over a century, there have been stories of Apache gold, a great gold mine with a location known only to the Apaches. They take what they need and only what they need. If anyone is thought to have betrayed the secret, that person dies, very suddenly. It is forbidden for the white man to ever know the secret. No one has ever proved the mine exists. Some have looked for it for years. Others say it is only a tale.'

'Perhaps that is the reason for this killing, perhaps not,' Aldama said.

'What do you want of us, Mr Aldama,' Thad asked.

Aldama answered. 'We need someone who is fearless, who can shoot as well or better than any of the company's hirelings. We want someone who can get to the bottom of this and return to us our way of life. The arrival of the men who sent Buck Hawkins and his monsters to hell has been taken as a sign from God.'

CHAPTER 7

Stunned by Aldama's statement, the three sat in awkward silence for what seemed a long time looking at one another.

'I never been sent anywhere by God before,' Rowdy stated in awe. 'It feels funny.'

'That's putting it mildly,' Coop said.

Thad finally shook off the surprise and said, 'Mr Aldama, we are just three young men who are on a personal mission of revenge. A man named Isaac Cripps murdered my parents in cold blood just a few days ago. The reason I am here is to travel to Jericho, hunt down Isaac Cripps and kill him. These are my two closest friends. They have chosen to come with me. Getting involved in a range war with a big faceless company is, to say the least, a long ways off our course from what we came here to do. This revenge we are after is dangerous enough without going up against professional killers.'

Aldama looked unhappy. 'We offer substantial pay for those who can help us,' he added with a note of hope in his voice.

'The pay is not important. . . .' Thad started, but Aldama interrupted him.

'Five hundred dollars apiece!'

'Damn!' Coop exclaimed.

'Dag gum!' Rowdy gasped.

'Did you make this offer to Hawkins?' Thad asked.

Aldama was shamefaced. 'Yes we did. It was like making a pact with Satan. Luckily, it was not generous enough. He wanted part of the land himself. We refused. He threatened but we remained firm and he finally left. But I felt he was more afraid than he was greedy.'

'Your offer is very generous, Mr Aldama,' Thad said. He looked at his two companions, obviously intrigued by the offer. 'We will let you know after we discuss it. Where can we reach you?'

'Don't be seen talking to me,' Aldama replied. 'You can send a note to me through Roy Fresquez, the deputy that you know.'

After Aldama left, the boys discussed the offer.

'We're getting off the trail,' Thad said. 'We came on this trip to kill Cripps, not to become hired guns.'

Coop answered, 'We know that and we haven't lost sight of it. But remember Thad, Rowdy and

79

I don't have property like you do. We live from hand to mouth. That much money would change our world completely. And don't tell me it wouldn't help you and Lila starting out.'

The expression on Thad's face told Coop his words had hit home and he pressed on. 'Let's find out who the key people are, find out what's ailing the sheriff and see if we can fix it. If we can, we make good money. If it's too big to fix, we move on and do what we came to do. After all, we aren't on a schedule of any kind.'

'I sure could use that money,' Rowdy said to no one in particular.

'Let's sleep on it,' Thad said. 'We'll decide at breakfast.'

The other two agreed and they slept on it.

The next morning, the three walked out of the hotel on their way to breakfast. As they started down the boardwalk to the café, three sour-looking men stepped into their path.

'Pardon me, sir,' Thad said to the man in front of him dressed as a nondescript trail hand.

The man did not move but stood regarding Thad, a twisted smile on his face. His bloodshot eyes stared out from under a heavy beetle brow accentuated by black bushy eyebrows.

'You were the boys talking to Aldama last night, weren't you?'

'What's it to you, stranger?' Thad said.

'I just want to give you a warning. You'll stay away from that crazy old man if you know what's good for you.'

'You have a big set of balls trying to tell me what I can and can't do,' Thad said. 'Who in the hell are you?'

'My name is Schwartz,' he growled. 'This fellow here is Strang,' he said tilting his head towards an unshaven and unkempt lout who had a big wad of tobacco in his mouth. Nodding toward a clean-shaven, neatly dressed man who wore a thin moustache and a superior attitude, he said, 'This is Benet.' He pronounced it 'Benay'. 'Want to know anything else?' Schwartz asked, taking an arrogant posture and folding his arms as if waiting for a reaction.

Thad suppressed a smile and asked, 'What are we supposed to do now? Wet our pants and run off down the street?'

The toughs looked startled.

The boys looked at the trio for a moment in silence then started laughing.

'If you birds have delivered your message, I suggest you get out of my way,' Thad said.

'You can't talk to us that way!' Strang spat.

'Oh yeh, I just did! Now get out of my way.'

With those words, Thad pushed Schwartz aside. From the corner of his eye, he saw Strang reach for his sidearm. Thad made his lightning draw and had the muzzle of his .44 pointed between Strang's eyes before the thug got the weapon halfway out. Startled, Strang released the pistol and raised his hands.

Thad and his friends went into the café where they had eaten supper the night before, laughing about the expression on Strang's face. The tall blond girl immediately came to their table, smiling at Rowdy.

Rowdy returned the smile. When she walked away, he said, 'Dag gum! She's nice.'

'Love sought is good, but love given unsought is better,' Coop said, grinning.

Rowdy nodded. 'I'll take it any way I can get it.'

After they had ordered and were sipping coffee, a fancy-dressed man approached the table. He wore a gold brocade vest under a blue coat. A heavy gold watch chain looped from one watch pocket to the other. His clothes were obviously of quality and impeccable. He sported a well-kept and heavily waxed moustache and his hair, visible under an expensive fedora, was heavily pomaded. He approached the table and said, 'Well gentlemen, I hear you turned down the offer to go to work for that bunch of local landowners, those that would hold back the future.'

Thad surveyed the dandy and answered, 'So?'

The dandy smiled and said, 'Wise choice. You

boys need to go back home and brand your cows or whatever you do. This business here is way above your level of experience and way too dangerous.'

'Well, thank you very much, my friend,' Thad said. 'You just put the final stamp on our decision. Your name is?'

'Nick Beale,' the man answered.

'How do you fit into all this business, Mr Beale?'

'Let's just say I'm the head facilitator.'

'For what company?'

Beale smiled. 'At the moment, a consortium of enterprises. We call it Comanche Holdings.'

Intrigued, Thad asked, 'What do you do when you get all the land you want?'

'Oh, well when that happens, then we sell the whole thing to a company and the several people involved divide the profits.'

'Of course,' Coop said. 'Then the original investors scatter to the four winds.'

'You've got it!' Beale said happily.

'And the new owner disclaims any involvement in the land acquisition process because he bought it all claim and lien free,' Coop added.

The smile faded noticeably from Beale's face. 'Once again, you have a good grasp of things,' he said warily.

Coop smiled in return.

'Will you be leaving soon?' Beale inquired almost casually.

'Yes, we will,' Thad answered in a flat, unemotional tone. 'We have some personal business to clear up, then we are happily on our way back home to brand our cows.'

Beale looked doubtful about Thad's tone, then put his smile back on. 'Well, fellows, have a good trip home.'

'Thanks,' Thad said as Coop and Rowdy nodded.

Beale exited the café with a proud strut, winking at Wynelle, the proprietress.

Coop said under his breath, 'The soul of this man is in his clothes.'

Rowdy frowned and said, 'I s'pose that's Shakespeare?'

Coop nodded.

Thad said in a low voice, 'I thought it couldn't get any worse than that clutch of saddle tramps we ran into on the way down here. But it has. Let's find Fresquez and get word to Aldama that we're going to work for him.'

Coop and Rowdy exchanged delighted smiles.

The craggy-faced Wynelle came to the table to refill the coffee cups.

'Ain't he the dandy one?' she commented.

Coop said, 'Did you get a big thrill when he winked at you.'

Wynelle cackled, showing some gaps where teeth had once been. 'If I was lookin' for a boy friend, which I ain't, I wouldn't pay that one no-never-mind anyhow. I figure that instead of getting a girl, he just stands in front of a mirror and plays with hisself.'

The boys had the best laugh they had known in days.

Fresquez told them that Aldama was delighted and that his prayers were answered. He gave instructions for a meeting that night at the home of a sheepherder. In case they were being watched, they were to ride out one at a time in three different directions then double back and follow a certain route to the meeting place.

Coop went first, then Rowdy and finally Thad. Thad was the last attendee to arrive and he found the others sipping strong coffee brewed by Senora Vasquez, wife of Fernando, the sheep-herder.

Aldama briefed them carefully on the members of the consortium's gang. There was Beale the boss, Peebles the bookkeeper, Ephram Strang and Bruno Schwartz, strong-arm men, and Auguste Benet, assassin and knife fighter. Aldama also suspected that another one or two were added to the payroll for certain special jobs but he did not know their names.

Thad proposed two actions for himself and his friends, to ferret out all information possible on the sheriff and attempt to discover the reason for his delaying and evasive actions, to act as watchmen when a homestead was threatened and to defend it with deadly force. What they learned as they probed local sources would lead them to the next step.

The next morning, Thad rode to the sheriff's office and went inside. He found Fresquez and another deputy tending the office. The other deputy went out on an errand and Thad pressed Fresquez.

'What has changed about the sheriff in the past few weeks?' Thad asked.

'He's been very nervous and on edge,' the deputy answered. 'He has been distracted, can't remember things and sometimes does not hear me when I'm talking to him.'

'Does he have a family?'

'Yes, his wife Maria, a boy called Pepe eleven years old and a beautiful little girl named Alma who is thirteen years old.'

'Have you seen them lately?'

'I saw Maria a few days ago. She looked terrible, like she had no sleep for days. The boy looked all right but he was very shy and withdrawn, not like himself at all.'

'How about the daughter?'

'No, I did not see her. When I asked about her, Maria was very evasive. This worries me greatly but I could not presume to question her.'

'Roy,' Thad said, 'if you wanted a dedicated man to do something against his principles, something even dishonest, how would you do it?'

'Threaten his life,' the deputy answered. 'But for a strongly moral man, threaten the life of someone dear to him.' Realization spread over Fresquez's face. 'Oh God!' he said.

'Does Alma have any friends?'

'Yes, Elena. Elena is her best friend.'

'Can you find her?'

'Let's go!'

The two rode to the sheriff's neighbourhood. As they rode into the street, they saw children playing. Fresquez said, 'There's Elena. Let me talk to her.'

Thad hung back as the deputy rode up to the girl and engaged her in conversation. In a few minutes, he said goodbye and rejoined Thad.

'She said she has not seen Alma in over two weeks,' the deputy said. 'When she went to Alma's house, the mother told her Alma had gone to visit her Tia* in Cruz.'

'Is that likely?' Thad asked.

Fresquez said, 'Elena said she had never heard

*Aunt

87

Alma mention an aunt. In fact, she said that Alma had once told her she had no aunts, only uncles. That's what she calls me, "Tio Roy".'

'That fits,' Thad said.

'You are thinking that someone has taken Alma and is holding her to make certain the sheriff co-operates,' Fresquez said, his voice growing thick with emotion.

'That's exactly what I'm thinking,' Thad answered. 'The next thing we have to do is find out where she is and get her back to her family. After that, we can work on the bully boys.'

'I am sick with fear for her, but I have to be careful,' Fresquez said. 'If they suspect I'm not staying under the thumb of the sheriff, I could be the next to be shot in the back.'

'You're right. I have been asking an awful lot of you,' Thad said. 'Go on about your job like it's any other day. I'll confront the sheriff myself.'

That night, the sheriff left his office at the usual time and rode home at a walk. Darkness had fallen by the time he reached his neighbourhood. He was a block from his home when another rider moved up alongside him. He looked at the rider but failed to recognize him.

'What do you want,' the sheriff asked warily.

'To get Alma back home and in your arms,' Thad said.

The sheriff reined to a stop. 'What are you talking about? Who are you?'

'Someone who is going to help you get your daughter back and rid your county of a plague,' came the answer.

'Go away!' The sheriff ordered, spurring his mount to a trot. 'You'll get my daughter killed.'

'No, I want to get her away from the people that have her so we can wipe out the rest of that vermin,' Thad said. 'You are in the middle of something you can't fight until your daughter is safe. Where is she?'

Once again, Sheriff Rogers stopped his horse. His head bent forward and his shoulders shook as he sobbed. Thad waited without speaking.

The sobs slowed and stopped. The sheriff said, 'I'm sorry about losing control like that.'

'Don't be,' Thad answered. 'You and your wife have been through absolute hell. It's time to end it. Where is she?'

'You're one of those Apache Wells men that killed Buck Hawkins and his gang, aren't you?'

'Yes, I am, along with my two associates.' The sheriff pulled himself up to his full sitting height and said in a clear voice, 'Jericho, that's where she is. A monster named John Burgoyne has her. He has orders to kill her if anyone tries to rescue her.'

'Then I'll make certain that John Burgoyne is

dead before he knows what I'm about.'

The sheriff sagged as if he were carrying the weight of the world on his back.

'If you can kill Hawkins, you can kill Burgoyne,' he said. 'I'll have to trust you. I can't live this way any longer and neither can my wife. Our lives are in your hands. Go get her.'

The sheriff nudged his mount and rode on to his house.

Back at the hotel, Thad walked into the room and said, 'Gentlemen, there's a damsel in distress we've got to rescue. We're heading for Jericho.'

CHAPTER 8

It was a hard thirty-mile ride across a desolate plain to the foothills outside Jericho. The Apache Wells trio stole into the hills not far from the notorious town in the late afternoon and Thad surveyed the place with his spyglass. They knew very little about Jericho. Deputy Fresquez had never been in Jericho and couldn't help them with their navigation around town.

They had no plan. They had no idea of where little Alma might be held, if indeed she were still alive. John Burgoyne reportedly was a ruthless killer who, like his friend Isaac Cripps, had no conscience and no discernible moral code. The chances that such a man would bother keeping a hostage alive were slim. They would have to gather data on the town and where Burgoyne would likely be.

Thad finished with his spyglass and turned to Rowdy. 'Rowdy, do you think you could be an

91

outlaw on the hideout from the law and drift into Jericho to find a place to nest for a while?'

Rowdy grinned broadly. 'I'd say I could do that without even thinking about it, Thad. What do you want me to do?'

'Drift into town,' Thad said. 'Go into a saloon and get a beer or drink or something and ask the bartender where you might put up for a night or two. If he gets curious, just tell him you escaped from gaol in Yucca and the law is looking for you and you've heard that the law doesn't visit Jericho very often.'

'Sounds reasonable,' Rowdy said.

'Don't rush it, but find out if Isaac Cripps is in town. Say you heard something in Yucca that he had passed through heading for Jericho, and that you remember your pappy talking about him a long time ago, when you were just a tad.'

'I can do that,' Rowdy said.

'And keep your ears open for any mention of John Burgoyne,' Thad added. 'He's the one that has the little girl. Be careful on that one, don't go asking around.'

Rowdy gathered his gear together and rode west to the road that connected Jericho and Amargosa. He looked in both directions at the road and saw no one so he turned right toward town.

As he rode into the edge of the small town, he

passed an unoccupied gallows. Rowdy idly wondered what crime a person might commit that would get him a hanging sentence in Jericho, since there was no law. He rode at a slow walk into the main part of town, a clutch of buildings on the west side of the road. Rowdy thought about it and realized it made sense. With the rear of the buildings to the west, the fronts and the irregular boardwalk that stretched in front of them would be sheltered from the western sun. In August, the sun in this part of the world was hellish.

Rowdy pulled up to what appeared to be a saloon. The paint on the front of the building was cracking and falling away. He could just make out the name of the place, 'The Horned Toad'. He watered Traveller at a wooden trough in front of the building then tied him to a hitching rail and walked into the saloon.

Rowdy noted that the saloon was not the most well appointed he had ever seen. The bar itself consisted of two planks about twelve feet long resting on empty barrels at either end. The table and chairs were crude and well used. A couple of often-missed brass spittoons provided the only attempt at class in the place.

Rowdy walked up to the bar and asked for a beer. The bartender pulled a beer and set it down in front of him. Rowdy put down a five-cent piece. The bartender, whose left ear consisted of some ragged flesh and a nasty-looking hole, squinted at Rowdy and said, 'You're short by ten cents.'

'What?' Rowdy squawked. 'Fifteen cents for a beer! I never paid more than a nickel anywhere.'

The bartender rasped, 'Fifteen cents or I take it back. This is Jericho, not a damned vacation resort like El Paso. It's hard to come by beer out here. Ya want it or not?'

'Seein' as how I'm about to die of thirst, I reckon I got no choice,' Rowdy said.

He drew two more nickels from his pocket and handed them over.

He took a swig of the beer and said, 'Did you just wring this out of a sick horse? Dag gum! If I'd knowed this was gonna taste like it had already been used, I'd have kept my fifteen cents.'

The bartender grimaced grotesquely in what apparently was a smile. Through amazingly gapped teeth he said, 'Ain't nobody holding a gun to your head, sonny.'

Rowdy swallowed the last of the beer and shook his head. 'Does the second one taste any better?'

'I think the stink lets up after the fourth or fifth one,' the bartender said, chuckling. 'Ready for another?'

'Might's well,' Rowdy replied. 'I ain't got the sand washed outta my craw yet.'

The bartender pulled another beer, collected another fifteen cents and leaned on the planks.

'Where'd ya come here from?' he asked.

'On up the line,' Rowdy answered. 'I was doin' pretty good till I hit Yucca. Dangdest town *I* ever saw! Some big ugly bird called me out and drew down on me because he thought I was a lawman looking for a friend of his. I had to shoot 'im, and then danged if I didn't get throwed in gaol.'

'That's a hell of a note!' the bartender said. 'What they charge you with?'

'Charged me with murder!' Rowdy replied. 'They was already planning the party they was gonna have at my hangin'. But they said it would be a fair trial.'

The bartender cackled shrilly and slapped his leg. 'Fair trial! That's a good one.'

A couple of curious idlers who had been sitting at a back table came up to the bar when the bartender started laughing.

'What's goin' on, Lop?' one of them said.

Still trying to get his laugher under control, Lop said, 'This feller got tossed in gaol up in Yucca for shootin' a man in a fair fight. He was about to tell me how he got outta there, ain't ya feller?'

Rowdy said, 'Why heck yes! That's the best part of the story.'

The idlers clustered around and the bartender pulled another beer for Rowdy.

'Well I'se just sitting there in that cell thinkin' I'd done come to the end of my trail,' Rowdy said. 'They was goin' to hang me for killin' that rascal when they shoulda give me a big dinner and a pocket watch with a gold fob. Heck fire! That town was a lot prettier without that ugly pile of buzzard guts in it.

'Anyway, I was just kind of foolin' with the end of that smelly little mattress on the bunk in that cell and there was a hole in it. I felt something stickin' out and it was the horsehair they had stuffed it with. Well sir, I pulled out a dab of that horsehair and it gave me an idea. I pulled a bunch outta there and kinda twisted it around and added some more to it and pretty soon I have what looked for all the world like a hairy spider that just about covered the palm of my hand. I twisted and trimmed a little on that thing then I put it in my pocket and started yelling for the deputy who was on duty. His name was Claunch and he wasn't too bright. I told him I was sick and about to shit in my trousers and I had to go to the outhouse. Their privy was in back of the gaol. Well anyway, he gripes a little but he didn't want the gaol all stinkin' so he let me out of the cell with his pistol on me and we went out back. I sat down on that privy and pulled the door halfway to and he kinda looked the other way and I yelled, "Oh God, what's that?" Then I hollered and shoved that door open and tossed that spider right at his face. Well sir, he screamed like your sister Fanny and started battin' at that fake spider and I hit him in the jaw with my fist and knocked him cold as last week's beans.'

Rowdy's audience roared its approval and Lop cackled loudly.

'Well,' Rowdy went on. 'I drug that old boy back inside and locked him in my cell. I took his keys and unlocked a cabinet and got my pistol outta there and my personal stuff out of a desk drawer where I saw that sheriff put it, then I went across the street to the stable where I'd left my horse. I got the hell outta Yucca and I don't think I's ever going back, 'cause if I do, that deputy will shoot me on sight.'

The idlers enjoyed Rowdy's tale and offered to buy him beers and he found that each one had his own story to tell. In another two hours, Rowdy had several comrades among the regulars at the Horned Toad Saloon.

One by one the others drifted away and Rowdy was left with Lop, the bartender. Rowdy started to ask where he might find a place to bunk for the night when Lop asked him, 'You said this dead gunslinger in Yucca thought you was a lawman?'

'That's what it sounded like to me the way he was carrying on, but I didn't even know what in the world he was talkin' about. I reckon he misunderstood when I was talkin' to the bartender in the saloon about a feller I used to know in Yucca named Isaac Gibbs and this ugly devil followed me outside. Funny looking citizen if I've ever seen one. Had one big eyebrow that went plumb across his firehead. Looked like a hairy snake. I reckon he thought I's talkin' about someone named Isaac somebody or other, I disremember now. Anyway, he wouldn't let me explain and started goin' for his iron. Darn! I didn't have no choice except to defend myself, and then them locals was gonna string me up for it!'

Rowdy put on his hat and said, 'Is there some place 'round here I can get a bunk for the night?'

'Yeah,' Lop replied. 'Right down the street. Prather place. House painted yellow. They rent out cots and throw in coffee and flapjacks the next morning. That is unless you'd rather bunk at Miss Lulu's whorehouse. You could kill two birds with one stone, so to speak.'

Rowdy threw his head back and laughed. 'Nope, I'll get my horns scraped another time.'

He started out of the door and said, 'Thanks Lop. Probably see ya tomorrow.'

'Wait!' Lop hollered. 'That name the feller you shot was askin' about, was it Isaac Cripps?'

Rowdy paused in the door. 'Yeah, I believe it was or somethin' like it. Like I say, the name didn't mean nothin' to me so I paid it no mind. Good night.'

The bartender watched the swinging doors swing to a stop after Rowdy went through then called to the back of the saloon, 'Clyde, watch the place for a while. I got to go see someone right quick.'

Rowdy made his way to the Prather place and arranged for a cot. The proprietor cautioned him that there was no smoking inside the place because of the danger of fire. As Prather put it, 'You dumb assed cowboys and gaol birds tie on the bear and then come here to sleep it off. First thing you know, you light up a damned "seegar" or one of them roll-yer-owns then go to sleep with it burning.'

Rowdy assured the proprietor that he did not use tobacco in any form cause his Momma always told him it was sinful. Properly enrolled, Rowdy put Traveller in the barn out back and got it fed. He then carried his bedroll and saddlebags into the sleeping room and found his assigned cot. It was one of ten arranged in close order side by side, five on each side of the room.

He spread his bedroll on the cot and sat down to take off his boots by the lantern light coming through the open door to the hallway. He heard someone clear his throat and he glanced around. It was Coop!

As pre-planned, Coop was pretending not to know Rowdy nor did Rowdy make any sign of recognition. Rowdy and Coop both settled down as best they could to get some sleep. Two of the residents were citizens of large proportions who started snoring. As their sleep deepened, the snoring increased in volume until it reached heroic proportions.

While Rowdy and Coop were trying to deal with the nocturnal noisemakers, Thad was several doors away to where he had followed Lop from the saloon. When Thad and Coop rode into town, Thad had seen Rowdy's horse tied up in front of the saloon. He told Coop to go on to find a place to lay their heads then set up a watch from a vantage point two doors down from the saloon. He had watched Rowdy leave and ride down the street to the flophouse. On a hunch, he waited for a few minutes and was rewarded by the sight of the one-eared bartender, still in his soiled bar apron, hurry down the street, obviously on a mission. Thad followed casually on his horse at a safe distance. The bartender approached a house on the edge of town and rapped on the door. The door opened and he was admitted.

Thad cantered past the house for a quarter mile then rode back at a walk. As he approached, the bartender re-emerged and hurried back to his post at the Horned Toad.

Thad watched the house for another ten minutes. The only light in the house went out and the place was dark. Thad waited a while longer but it appeared that whoever the bartender visited wasn't going out tonight.

Thad nudged Cochise and headed for the boarding house.

The next morning, the boarding house residents were putting away the Prather flapjacks when a tough-looking bruiser walked in and asked, 'Is there a Rowlett Mason in this bunch?'

The men glanced around to see who was going to respond. After a few seconds, Rowdy stood up.

'What's it to ya stranger?' he asked.

'Mr Crown wants to see you,' he responded.

'Who in heck is Mr Crown?' Rowdy growled in a loud voice.

The tough-looking bruiser looked irritated and started to speak but Prather interrupted.

'He runs this town, pilgrim. He's the law. I wouldn't keep him waiting,' Prather said.

'Well my, my,' Rowdy said to the room in

general, 'maybe he's heard how pretty I am and he's going to give me a job.'

There was a chorus of laughter and Rowdy chewed his last flapjack, put on his hat, picked up his gear and followed the messenger out the door. The messenger had a buckboard in the street and Rowdy tossed his gear into the bed and climbed into the seat. Thad drifted outside and watched the buckboard pull to a stop a block away next door to the saloon. Rowdy and the messenger stepped down and walked into an office.

Thad and Coop looked at one another and Thad said, 'Rowlett?'

They walked down the street slowly, trying not to attract attention. They walked past the office into which Rowdy had disappeared and stopped when they reached the saloon. They leaned against a couple of posts holding up the part of the roof that extended over the boardwalk. After another ten minutes, Rowdy walked out of the office smiling. He saw his friends but made no sign of recognition and walked into the saloon. Thad waited a few minutes, then turned and walked into the saloon. Rowdy was standing by the bar, drinking a beer. Thad walked up and leaned against the bar a few feet away from Rowdy and ordered a beer.

Thad took a sip of his beer and reacted to the

bitter flavour as had Rowdy. Rowdy laughed and said, 'Say there, stranger, must be the first time you tried that beer.'

Thad answered, 'Is this really beer or did he draw me some panther piss?'

'Naw, no panthers,' Rowdy answered. 'After the first half dozen or two, they get to tastin' pretty good.'

Lop the bartender overheard the conversation and joined it. 'You think that the beer is bad, wait till you taste the whiskey!' He laughed a high-pitched cackle at his own cleverness.

'What is it?' Coop chimed in. 'Comanchero whiskey left over from the Indian trade?'

Lop looked surprised and then cackled loudly. 'That's good, stranger. But the Injuns been gone for a long time now. It ought to be aged down nice and mellow, but it ain't, so it can't be Comanchero whiskey.' He cackled again.

Coop tilted his hat back on his head and said, 'I was thinking of getting something to warm my insides but after hearing you pilgrims talk about the beer and whiskey, I think I'll just have a sas'prilla.'

Lop finally talked Coop into having a gin, reassuring him that he had some genuine British gin and everyone knew that the British were particularly adept at distilling gin.

As the three were drinking their drinks, Lop said, 'Hey Mason, why don't you tell the boys about how you got out of the gaol at Yucca?'

Rowdy told Lop that was a good idea but he wanted to sit down for a while. The three moved to a table where Rowdy told his spider escape story again. After the laughs had settled down Thad leaned forward and spoke in a low voice.

'Who is that Mr Crown that summoned you?' he asked.

Rowdy said 'Hiram Crown is the stud duck of this whole dad blasted operation! He runs Jericho. He's the sheriff and the judge and jury. That story I just told you, I told last night here at the bar. I reckon that someone went and told him about it, 'cause when I walked in his office, the first jack out of the box he was askin' about Yucca and the man I killed, that is, the man Thad killed. He allowed as how Mr Cripps was goin' to be mighty unhappy bout his man in Yucca gettin' killed.'

'Is he a friend of Cripps?' Thad asked.

'I don't think they were bosom friends, maybe business partners,' Rowdy answered. 'I asked Crown, "Yo goin' to tell Cripps that I croaked his man?" and he sad, "When the timing suits my purpose".'

'What does that mean?' Coop asked.

'Danged 'f I know,' Rowdy answered.

Thad said, 'Sounds to me that he's got something on you he can use. Did he ask you to do anything?'

'Nope. Not a thing,' Rowdy replied.

'Have you heard anything about Cripps or where he might be?' Thad asked.

'Not a dad gum thing,' Rowdy replied. 'The only . . . hold it a minute.'

Rowdy looked over at Lop and asked, 'Lop, what was that name you asked me about last night?'

'Cripps,' the bartender replied.

'Does he live around here?' Rowdy asked.

'Yep, sure does, on down south of town. Lives in a little adobe that his friend Burgoyne and a Mexican woman live with him. Don't ask me about that bunch. I don't know a thing,' Lop said, rolling his eyes.

'Thanks Lop,' Rowdy said. 'Just trying to get the lay of the land round here.'

Coop said, nodding. 'Well that's one way to find out what you want to know. Ask somebody.'

'Danged if it didn't work!' Rowdy said.

'Looks like I'm going to be snooping around tonight,' Thad said.

'Don't you want any help?' Coop asked.

'At a safe distance. We're taking a big enough risk with just one of us snooping around there.'

Coop looked around to make sure they

weren't being overheard. 'You think that's where they have the girl?'

'If she's still alive, yes,' Thad answered.

'Then it's tonight,' Coop said.

'Tonight,' Thad repeated.

It had been dark for two hours when Thad and Coop rode south out of town toward the adobe where Cripps lived. The flat terrain made it impractical to take up a post nearby to watch the house in the daytime. So they had ridden past earlier in the day and saw the woman out back washing clothes in a washtub. When they had returned later, she was hanging them out to dry. No one else was visible.

Thad stopped and dismounted about one hundred yards short of the house. He led his horse off the road and tied it to a mesquite tree. Coop rode on past the house and stopped about seventy-five yard past on the other side. He too led his mount off the road and tied it up.

Rowdy rode up to where Thad was waiting and dismounted. He held the reins of both horses. Thad started toward the house, staying off the road and at a right angle to it until he was fifty or so yards farther from the road than was the adobe. He then turned parallel with the road and walked to a point in the desert behind the house. From there, he approached the adobe carefully a few steps at a time. They had not seen a dog when they rode by earlier, a factor in Thad's willingness to spy on the house itself under cover of darkness.

It was a moonless night, Thad observed, well suited for mischief. He knew there was a shed behind the house for the horses. Close by was a chicken coop. He would have to avoid both.

He approached the house slowly. There was a water well a hundred paces from the back door and there was the danger that someone would come out of the house to get water and see him. As he approached the house, his eyes were on the back door. He scurried across the level and open ground near the house to the south side. Anyone coming out the back door would not be able to see him.

Thad approached a window set at the centre of the south wall. He flattened himself against the wall and listened. He heard movement inside, the sounds of domesticity, plates and eating utensils, voices saying things he could not distinguish. He heard the woman speak and a man's voice answering. Then his hair stood on end; he heard a child's thin wavering voice, a young female, speaking in Spanish. A man's voice, harsh and abrupt, silenced the girl.

There was another male voice, sharp-edged,

angry. Then Thad heard the movements of two people in the room with the window. They started arguing.

'Why in hell don't you get rid of that brat? She's nothing but a pain in the ass.'

The second voice said, 'Maria has gotten fond of the girl. I'd never hear the end of it if I got rid of her.'

The first voice said, 'God damn, John! You going to let that woman tell you what to do? Why hell, I'll kill both of 'em right now for you and we'll have that pain-in-the-ass out of our way. That dumb-assed sheriff in Amargosa won't know the difference. He'll think she's still alive until it's too late.'

'Shut the hell up!' the second voice said. 'If anyone kills the girl, it will be me. I'll break her neck so it will be quick, not that crazy shit with the knife you like so much. Besides, I like having Maria around. This is my house anyway.'

The first voice came back, 'Don't let your big damned mouth overload your lazy ass, John.'

'Don't be worrying about that little girl. You've got Crown to deal with.'

'You mean we, don't you, John?'

'We're biting off an awful lot, Isaac. If that bastard finds out what we . . .'

They were walking out of the room so Thad couldn't understand the rest of what was said except it included the phrase 'staked out on an ant hill'.

Thad had what he came for and more. 'Time to get out of this place and do some serious planning,' he said to himself.

He learned the girl Alma, was still alive. He also learned that as long as Cripps was associated with Burgoyne, the girl's life was in danger.

He retraced his steps away from the house and out into the darkness. He heard a door open and he fell to the ground. He turned his head slightly and looked back. He could see someone standing outside the back door looking right and left and peering in his direction. The man's arm was held in a position that looked as if he had a gun in his hand.

CHAPTER 9

Thad lay motionless. The seconds ticked by and he felt perspiration rolling down his neck, under his chin where it dropped into the sand. He heard a scurrying close to his face. It was a large scorpion, hunting its prey in the night. The creature sensed Thad and knowing such a mass represented danger, scurried in another direction. Thad heard many subtle noises in the darkness, other small creatures going about their business.

Thad tucked his chin down so he could see behind him. The man stood motionless, looking in Thad's direction. He guessed from the size of him, it was John Burgoyne. Thad knew that at this distance and on a dark night, it would be virtually impossible for Burgoyne to make out a coherent shape lying motionless on the ground.

Finally, Burgoyne let his right hand drop to his side. Satisfied that whatever was out there was gone, he turned and went back into the house.

Thad lay motionless a while longer. His instinct served him well for the door burst open again and the big man lurched into the back yard of his adobe and scanned the desert again. Even in the darkness, he would have been able to see a grown man running across the sand and Alma's life would be forfeit.

For a long period, Burgoyne scanned the desert, then apparently satisfied, went back into the house. Thad got to his feet and scurried away in a crouch. At the edge of Jericho, the trio stopped and moved off the road to talk. Thad related to Coop and Rowdy what he had over-heard through the window. He added, 'We can't waste any time.'

'I'm with you, Thad,' Coop said. 'It's got to be tomorrow at the latest.'

Rowdy nodded agreement. 'Then we have to get them out of that house. If we tried to take her while one of them is there . . .' Thad said.

'We have to get Cripps and Burgoyne away from the house. The woman shouldn't be much of a problem,' Coop said.

'Let's work on that idea. What's the best way to do that?' Thad asked.

'Let's get back where we can sit and talk,' Coop said.

'The saloon?' Rowdy suggested.

*

They got beer and sat at a corner table. Lop looked at them curiously when they walked in but he soon turned his attention to other matters.

Thad counted off their choices on his fingers.

'First, we get them both out of the house on some pretext, and one of us grabs the girl and rides like hell for Amargosa. Second, we could kill both of them and grab the girl if we can get her away from the old lady.' Thad paused, and then continued, 'Maybe we can pull this off, two birds with one stone.' Thad watched Lop working behind the bar. He got up and walked over to the bar and motioned to Lop. The bartender walked over to Thad and leaned across the bar to hear what he had to whisper into the good ear. Then Thad returned to the table.

'I told him when he got to a stopping place to come over and join us because we had a big problem we needed to ask him about.'

In a few minutes, Lop motioned to his assistant and came out from behind the bar. He walked to the table and sat down.

In a hushed voice, Thad said, 'You know Mr Crown pretty well, don't you Lop?'

The bartender said with a touch of pride, 'Yes, I do. Mr Crown depends on me for a lot of information.'

112

'Good,' Thad said. 'Here's what I want him to find out about. I understand that Isaac Cripps and John Burgoyne have a kidnapped child out at Burgoyne's place. She's thirteen years old and she's the daughter of the Cudahey County sheriff.'

Lop's bloodshot eyes seemed to bulge in surprise. 'Holy Mother!' he exclaimed.

Thad went on. 'We picked up the story in Amargosa. Tonight, I confirmed that the girl is out there. If anything happens to her, God help Jericho! They'll be out here with an army and burn the place down.'

Lop looked genuinely distressed. 'I think I better pass this along right now.'

Lop got up, went behind the bar and had a hurried conversation with his assistant, then scurried out.

In fifteen minutes, Lop bustled back into the bar. He was perspiring heavily and wiping at his face with his apron as he approached Thad's table.

'Mr Crown wants to see you right away,' he said to Thad.

'How about these fellows?' Thad asked, nodding toward his partners.

'Just you,' Lop answered. 'Do you know where to go?'

'Yep,' Thad answered, getting to his feet. 'Be

back in a while, boys.'

Thad walked next door to Crown's office. He rapped on the door and waited. A big cowboy opened the door and looked at Thad.

'What's your name?' he demanded.

'Thad Forrester'

'Come in and I'll take your sidearm,' the burly man said.

Thad pulled his .44 from its holster and handed it to the man butt first.

Thad followed the big man into the interior of the building. In sharp contrast to the rest of the town, the place was well appointed. The walls were panelled with dark, lustrous wood set off by tasteful paintings in decorous frames. The furniture was rich-looking and of the finest craftsmanship. Rugs of an origin unknown to Thad were strategically placed on the polished hardwood floor. The interior of the place was completely out of keeping with the rest of Jericho. Thad mentally likened it to an innocent schoolgirl from an exclusive eastern finishing school being plunked down in the red light district of Juarez.

The big man ushered Thad into the main office in the back. Behind a large mahogany desk sat a distinguished-looking gentleman with greying temples and wearing what appeared to Thad to be a very expensive suit of clothes. He was smoking a cigar.

The man looked at Thad in an appraising manner and said, 'My name is Hiram Crown. I run this town.'

'Pleased to meet you, Mr Crown. I'm Thad Forrester, from Apache Wells,' Thad said.

Crown gestured to a chair that faced the big desk and Thad sat down.

Crown blew a big puff of smoke into the air and said, 'Lop has brought me some unwelcome news. Such a thing could be awkward for several people . . . if it's true.'

'If you're talking about the kidnapped thirteen year-old, it's true enough,' Thad said. 'I have no reason to lie to you nor do I have the very poor judgment to do so.'

'You know personally that the girl is being kept at Burgoyne's,' Crown asked, eyeing Thad closely.

'Yes sir, I do. I confirmed it myself this very night.'

'Why are you in Jericho?' Crown asked.

'Two reasons,' Thad began. 'The first is to free the girl and get her safely back to Amargosa.'

'And the second?'

'To kill Isaac Cripps,' Thad said in a normal tone.

There was a heavy silence in the room for several seconds. Crown looked at Thad through narrowed eyes and finally spoke.

'You know of course that Cripps is under my protection here in Jericho.'

'I know that.'

Crown leaned forward, squinting at Thad. 'I'll say this, young man, you are either crazy or you've got *huevos** the size of whiskey barrels, and you don't talk like you're loco. Pray tell why do you wish ill toward poor Cripps?'

In the same even tone, Thad said, 'A few days ago, shortly after he was released from prison, Cripps came to Apache Wells to take revenge on the lawman that captured him and sent him to prison. That man was my father. Cripps came to the front door and knocked like any visitor. When my mother opened the door, he shot her. When my father rushed in, Cripps shot him. With his dying breath, my father told me who shot him and my mother and where to find him.'

'Why should I have any sympathy toward an old lawman?' Crown asked, leaning back in his leather chair.

'No reason,' Thad replied. 'But you do have a concern for one of your people doing something that will bring the wrath of the whole state down on your neck. How long do you think you could hold off an army of sheriffs and deputies

* Eggs, Mexican slang for testicles.

116

backed up by the Texas Rangers? Moreover, you do have a practical reason to eliminate someone who has his eye on that chair you're sitting in.'

Crown was startled. He slammed his hand down on the desk and shouted, 'How do you know that?'

'I overheard Cripps and Burgoyne discussing their plans. You just confirmed that you knew about it as well,' Thad said.

Crown got out of his chair and paced back and forth behind it.

'You know a hell of a lot for a young squirt,' he said. He paced some more then spoke again.

'What do you want, Forrester?'

Thad leaned forward in his chair. 'Two things,' he said. 'Send for Cripps and Burgoyne, have them here in the morning, say ten o'clock. That will allow my man to get the girl out of Burgoyne's house unharmed and take her back to her family. Then let me call Cripps out in a fair fight. I'll make sure that everyone knows why I'm calling him out, so it's between me and him and you're clean. Then I'll kill him. He's out of the way, your hands are clean, and you don't have to worry about the army coming after you.'

Crown paced a couple more times and stopped. 'We'll do it. But what if he kills you?'

Thad smiled. 'Half your problem goes away with the girl safely back home. Cripps would still be your problem. But looking at this place, I think you are resourceful enough to handle it.'

Crown extended his hand.

Back in the saloon, Thad went over the plan with Rowdy and Coop

'Rowdy,' he said. 'I want you to be shadowing the Burgoyne house in the morning from a safe distance or hiding place of some kind. When Burgoyne and Cripps leave to come into town, go to the house and get the little girl. Try not to hurt the lady that's keeping her. Then ride like hell for Amargosa. Better take water for Traveller as well as yourself and Alma and probably something to eat. I want you to do it because you're the best rider among us and the strongest.'

Rowdy nodded.

'Coop, I want you to stay here to watch my back. I don't know what kind of trick Cripps may pull out of his ass. Got it?'

'Got it,' Coop said.

'Now,' Thad went on. 'Crown has sent a man to Burgoyne's tonight to tell him to be in Crown's office by ten o'clock. That means those two will have to leave the house by about half past nine to be on time.'

The three left the saloon and walked to the boarding house hoping they could get a little sleep.

*

Rowdy found a good place for watching Burgoyne's adobe. There was a dry wash three or four hundred yards from the house where Rowdy found he could hide the horse from anyone on the road. He lay at the edge of the wash where he could stick his head up, after removing his hat, and get a good view of the adobe. He had slept fitfully and finally abandoned the attempt and took up his station early.

Finally, he saw the door open and two men came out hatless and went to the shed that sheltered their horses. After fifteen minutes or so, they both returned to the house. Rowdy assumed they had bridled and saddled their mounts for the ride into town. Another wait followed, then the two emerged. One was wearing a hat. The other had what appeared to be a blue bandana tied around his head. The big one paused and turned back to the house. From his gestures, he was giving last minute instructions to the woman that lived with him and took care of Alma. The men led their mounts out of the shed into the yard, mounted up and rode away to the road and settled into an easy lope.

When they were a safe distance down the road, Rowdy mounted up and rode the horse up out of the dry wash and headed directly for the house. He pulled up at the back of the house and went to the door. He tried the door and it opened. He walked in and heard a voice from another room. The woman, Maria, appeared suddenly, saw him and screamed. She turned and ran into another room and Rowdy followed. As he expected she had led him directly to the girl. The woman was attempting to hide Alma behind her skirts. When Rowdy reached for her, the woman grabbed her up and held on fiercely.

Rowdy understood why Roy Fresquez was so fond of the child. She was beautiful with long jet-lack hair, large dark innocent eyes and a flawless tea-coloured complexion.

Rowdy took the child from the woman and said, 'Alma, I am taking you to your father.'

Alma threw her arms around his neck.

'Is there anything you want to take with you?' he asked.

She shook her head vigorously and Rowdy headed for the door. The woman followed screaming in Spanish and pounding with her small fists on his back. Rowdy strode out the back door, set Alma on the horse behind the saddle and mounted himself. He kicked his spurs into the horse, clicked his tongue and they left at a full gallop.

In Jericho, Cripps and Burgoyne rode up to Crown's office next door to the saloon, dismounted and tied up their horses. They walked through the front door and handed their weapons to Crown's big assistant. They stepped into the inner office, removed their hats and waited for Crown to notice them. Finally, he turned around, smiled and gestured to two chairs in front of his desk.

After they sat and made themselves comfortable, Crown started to speak.

'What's this I hear about a little thirteen year old girl staying with you chaps out at your house Burgoyne?'

Burgoyne jumped to his feet and yelled, 'Who told you that?'

Crown fixed him with an icy stare. 'Sit down, you dimwit! I'm asking the questions.'

Burgoyne realized the extent of his transgression and sat back down, looking sheepish.

Looking at the ash on his cigar, Crown asked, 'What did you have to do with this Cripps?'

Cripps, anxious to put space between himself and Burgoyne answered, 'When I got back here after the state cut me loose, John already had this thing with the kid going on. He made a deal with some folks over in Amargosa to hide the kid.'

'John,' Crown said, 'Did it occur to you that such a thing is forbidden here in Jericho? We have a tacit arrangement with the law. We stay within certain limits and the law doesn't bother us. Now, you have kidnapped a thirteen year-old female and carried her to Jericho. How do the people in Amargosa who are concerned about the girl feel about that? They might ask, "Are they raping the little girl? Are they doing horrible things to her?" ' Crown stood behind his desk. 'They might even go so far as to form an army to come over here and get her and burn down the town in the process! *Did that ever occur to you, Burgoyne?*' he shouted.

Burgoyne shifted uncomfortably and looked at the floor. 'But nobody was supposed to know,' he said almost tearfully.

Suddenly, Burgoyne realized that if Crown knew about the child, someone else knew. If someone else knew and came for the child and returned her to her parents, the people who contracted with him would be extremely unhappy!

Burgoyne jumped to his feet.

Crown yelled 'Sit down!'

Burgoyne turned and ran out of the office with Crown's shouts echoing in his ears. He jumped on his horse and spurred it unmercifully, heading back toward the adobe at full speed.

Crown looked down the street at Burgoyne rapidly disappearing in the distance and walked back in to his office shaking his head. Cripps sat there in his chair, unmoved. As Crown sat down behind his desk, Cripps said, 'I been trying to get John to kill that kid and the old gal that lives with him. They both are pains in the ass. The old gal has him whipped down though and he wouldn't listen to me.'

'Isaac,' Crown said, 'Why in the name of all that's holy did you commit a murder just as soon as you got paroled? It was a revenge killing at that; it served no practical purpose except to get people looking for you, and here you are in our snug little community. Oh yes, I forgot. You killed a woman too, a defenceless woman, in her own home. Then you came straight here while people were taking vows to track you down and kill you.'

Cripps squirmed in his chair. 'It was like this,' he said. 'That sheriff beat me within an inch of my life, right there in the middle of the street with them yokels laughing at me. I coulda took it if he'd shot me dead right then, but he didn't. That big asshole beat me up so bad I couldn't eat for two weeks and I pissed blood for a month. For fifteen years I sat in that shit hole just thinking about getting even with that son of a bitch. Fifteen years! It was something that had to be done.'

'That's interesting Cripps,' Crown said. 'You

killed the sheriff that whipped your ass and you killed his wife for good measure. Did you think you were just going to ride away and everybody would forget about it?'

'Who is going to follow me here and try to do something about it?' Cripps sneered.

'We'll see, won't we?' Crown asked.

Burgoyne reached his modest adobe and leaped out of the saddle and ran into the house. Maria was sitting at the table weeping.

'What happened?' Burgoyne roared.

'The man came and took Alma,' she said in Spanish. 'He knocked me down and picked her up and went out and got on a horse and rode away.'

'You stupid bitch!' Burgoyne yelled. He grabbed her by the hair and pulled her from the chair.

"Which way did he go?' he demanded while she screeched with pain.

'The North,' she whined.

Burgoyne hurled her to the floor. He rummaged around in a cabinet and pulled out a pistol. He loaded and holstered it and ran back to his horse. He quickly mounted and rode north at full speed.

Back in town, Crown was saying, 'Let's go next door and have a drink.'

'Yeh, sure,' Cripps answered, relieved.

Trailed by Crown's burly assistant, they walked from the office to the boardwalk and immediately turned into the Horned Toad. Thad and Coop were sitting on chairs tilted back against the wall in front, watching the passers-by.

No sooner than Crown and Cripps sat down at a table than Lop brought them a special bottle and two small glasses.

They had kept the fast pace for a long time. Jericho had faded in the distance behind them and Rowdy allowed the horse to slow to a walk.

'Are you thirsty?' he asked Alma.

She nodded in reply and he reached for his canteen and opened it for her. She drank big gulps, wiped her mouth and smiled at him. He took several long swigs and put the stopper back in. He looked at the sun. It was directly overhead. He would stop in an hour or so and they would have something to eat.

Cripps was delighted that his disciplinary session seemed to have ended and he sat with Crown in the Horned Toad saloon and sipped a fine brandy that Lop kept exclusively for the big boss. Cripps was at first relaxed, but he became increasingly uneasy. Not only was Crown more smug than usual, he was more condescending than usual. On occasion, he smiled to himself for no apparent reason. He seemed to be waiting for something.

Crown called over his assistant who bent over and listened as his boss whispered in his ear. The big man nodded and walked out the front door.

The assistant walked up to Coop and Thad and said, 'Anytime now'. Then he tapped Coop on the shoulder and motioned for him to follow. Coop looked questioningly at Thad who nodded. He then followed the big man inside to Crown's table.

Crown said, 'Cripps, this is Coop. He's going to sit with me for a while.' Both Cripps and Coop looked mystified at the words.

Thad walked into the street and faced the saloon. In a booming voice he yelled, 'Isaac Cripps! I'm calling you out. You are a cowardly son of a bitch. What do you say, Cripps? I'm waiting.'

Cripps sat dumbfounded during Thad's challenge and paled visibly. He looked at Crown wide-eyed with fear. When he saw the expression of triumph on Crown's face, he knew he had been led into a trap.

Crown said, 'Well, Cripps. Do you have the guts?'

Cripps snarled. 'You no-good son of a bitch! You set this up.'

Crown put on an expression of mock amazement. 'Why Cripps, whatever do you mean?'

The voice came from outside again. 'Well Cripps. Are you coming out?'

Thad stood in the street watching the swinging doors and waiting. People were starting to gather to watch the show. Cripps stared at Crown for several moments then got to his feet unsteadily. He squared his shoulders and attempted a confident walk to the door. He paused just inside the swinging doors and drew himself to his full height then stepped outside.

Crown turned to Coop and said, 'Let's go watch the show.'

The big man removed Coop's pistol from its holster and stuck it in his belt. He took Coop's arm and grasped it firmly as they walked outside and stood on the boardwalk.

Cripps stepped into the street eyeing Thad carefully.

Thad smiled as Cripps reached the street. He said, 'My name is Thad Forrester. You shot and killed my mother while she was standing on her own doorstep. After you shot her, you shot my father who was unarmed and trying to protect the wife he had been married to for twenty-two years. Now I'm giving you the chance to kill the last one in the family.'

Cripps stood staring at Thad with a twisted smile and trying to keep his hands from trembling.

Crown called from the boardwalk, 'Forrester, I've got your man Coop here. I wanted to let you know that if Cripps kills you, my man will kill Coop in the way of cleaning things up. If you kill Cripps, he goes free. Understand?'

The assistant pulled his six-shooter and put it by Coop's head, cocking the hammer.

Thad glanced at Coop and gave a quick, tight smile to reassure him, then his eyes went back to Cripps. He felt ice drop into his stomach.

'I understand,' he said. To his satisfaction, his voice was even. Then he said, 'It's your move, Isaac Cripps.'

Crown lit one of his cigars. He blew a cloud of smoke into the air and smiled.

CHAPTER 10

Thad said, 'Cripps, the first one is for my mother, the next one is for my father and the third one is for some poor soul you killed that I never heard of.'

Cripps' face twisted into a grotesque caricature of a human and his arm dropped to his holster.

Thad knew that Crown's move with Coop was designed to rattle him and he had to push everything out of his mind and concentrate on what he had to do. His hand went to his Colt and his forefinger to the trigger; he started the pressure, not too much, and drew the weapon. He brought the barrel up and aligned it with Cripps, keeping the pressure. There was the critical moment and he knew the barrel pointed at Cripps' chest. Keep the pressure smooth and *now*!

Thad's shot hit Cripps on the right side of his chest and spun him to the right. Cripps' shot hit a bystander in the leg. He turned back and tried to bring his weapon up to bear on Thad. Thad fired again and hit him in the stomach. The impact bent Cripps over and the pain blinded him. His hand tightened on the trigger and he fired one more shot that went into the ground. Thad's third shot smashed through his breast-bone and shattered his spine. He crumpled into a heap in the dirt, dead before he fell.

Crown's assistant let down the hammer of his weapon and returned his six-shooter to its holster. Then he returned Coop's long-barrel pistol to him. Coop sat down on the edge of the boardwalk to let the fluttering in his stomach quit.

The crowd pressed around Cripps' body, marvelling at the placement of Thad's shots. Thad holstered his .44 and walked up to Crown, glancing at a highly relieved Coop.

Thad said, 'I suppose our business here is finished up, Mr Crown. Me and Coop will be moseying back to Apache Wells now.'

'Sure you won't stay a while?' Crown said. 'This is a real friendly town.'

'We don't want to outstay our welcome,' Thad replied. 'But it's been a real pleasure.'

Thad and Coop walked back to the boarding house to get their gear and horses. Thad's hands trembled a bit but it wasn't noticeable to anyone else.

As they prepared to leave, Coop noticed that Thad was unusually quiet.

'Something wrong?' he asked.

Thad was silent for a moment then he said, 'It wasn't like I thought it would be, Coop. I thought there would be this big joy or at least some kind of relief. But there wasn't. I just got a little bit sick to my stomach again. I've dreamed of killing that man for days; I could hardly think of anything else and made that my sole purpose in life. But you know what, Coop?'

'No, what?'

'I was thinking of that thirteen-year-old girl and it came to me that . . .'

'That what, Thad?'

'That it was more important to get that little girl back home alive than it was to kill Isaac Cripps. Cripps was just pathetic.'

Coop thought for a moment. He finally said, 'I think that proves you're a decent person, Thad. You could have ignored those folks and their troubles, but you couldn't and when that dandy, what's his name, Beale, rubbed you the wrong way, that was your excuse to get involved, wasn't it?'

Thad smiled a thin smile to himself because Coop understood his motivation.

Coop stepped into his saddle and leaned over to whisper to Othello. 'Let's get the hell out of this crazy town.'

Othello snorted, a sound that could have been taken for disgust.

Burgoyne realized he had made a terrible mistake. He had no water for himself or his horse and he knew the only water hole between Amargosa and Jericho was a mile and a half from the road. He hoped his horse could keep up the pace because if he didn't kill the girl and her rescuer before they reached Amargosa, he was as good as dead himself. He pushed on through the heat.

Rowdy gave himself and Alma a break by reining to a halt by a roadside shrine. He took Alma's arms and lowered her to the ground, then climbed out of the saddle. The shrine provided enough space for a small person to sit down some place other than the sand. When Rowdy filled his canteen the night before, he bought some tortillas and a few baked sweets. He chewed on a tortilla and gazed back down the road. He took a swig from the canteen and filled the horse's canvas drinking bag from the bag of water that accompanied his saddlebags.

Alma said that she was getting sore from riding behind him astride the big horse so after he stowed everything back in its place, he climbed into the saddle, took her by the hands

132

and pulled her into the saddle in front of him where she could ride side-saddle like 'one of those snooty Eastern ladies,' he said. She smiled and settled down. Soon she was asleep against his chest.

John Burgoyne expected his horse to drop dead at any moment. His own throat was parched and raw and he knew he would kill for a drink of water. He stared ahead hoping in vain to see a man on horseback with the child. Heat distorted the road and the horizon, playing tricks. He thought he saw a man riding a horse on a path at a right angle to his. The vision disappeared as the heat waves wavered and fluctuated, teasing him. The vision appeared again, indistinctly. Was it close or was it far away? He knew it could be miles away. It wavered out of sight then reappeared again. It was real! There really was a man on horseback walking the horse slowly to the road. Burgoyne kept his eyes on the rider scarcely blinking, afraid that if he lost sight of it for even a moment, it would disappear into the air again.

He rode on and the rider and horse finally reached the road. The rider turned to the right, toward Amargosa, but turned in his saddle and looked back at Burgoyne. He reined his mount to a stop and watched the man and half-dead horse approach. Burgoyne finally reached the rider, stopped his horse and climbed out of his saddle.

The rider said, 'My friend, you don't look very good.'

Burgoyne said, 'Do you have water?'

'I wouldn't be out here without it,' the rider said, reaching for his canteen.

Burgoyne took the canteen and drank eagerly, taking great gulps.

The rider asked,' You need anything else?'

Burgoyne put the stopper back in the canteen, reached up and took the horse's bridle and said, 'Yes, your horse.'

The rider started to speak in protest when Burgoyne drew and shot him. Burgoyne held on to the bridle as the startled horse reared and the rider fell from his saddle. The killer walked around the horse and went through the dead man's pockets, taking what cash he could find. He then mounted the fresh horse and spurred it to a gallop toward Amargosa.

Rowdy and Alma saw Amargosa in the distance and they knew they had only a few miles to go. Traveller was moving at a trot and Rowdy wanted to spur him to a gallop but they already had covered thirty miles and he didn't want to punish the animal any more than he had to. He looked back along the route they had taken. At first he didn't see anything then a distant movement caught his eye. The heat distorted distant things so he couldn't be sure. But just in case, he spurred the horse to an easy lope.

Alma noticed the faster pace and Rowdy turning to look back.

'What's wrong?' she asked.

'Probably nothing,' he answered, 'I'm just in a hurry to get my supper.'

In another five minutes Rowdy looked back again. He could see that it was a man on horseback, riding hard. He spurred Traveller to a gallop.

Thad and Coop kept their mounts going at a trot. They rode north without conversation. Coop saw that Thad was exhausted and nearly asleep in the saddle. The morning's tension had taken its toll.

When Thad became a little more alert, Coop asked, 'You think we ought to camp tonight?'

'No,' replied Thad. 'I'm worried about Rowdy and the girl. I figure Burgoyne went after them.'

'Since we haven't seen anything of him, I reckon you're right,' Coop responded.

Thad said, 'Let's hope the next time we see him, he's in gaol or dead.'

'I'll go along with that,' Coop chortled.

'What's that up ahead?' Thad said.

Coop squinted up the road. 'That's a horse by the side of the road.'

'That's not all,' Thad murmured, half to himself. He drew his pistol and spurred his horse to a lope and Coop followed.

They found the horse beside the road attempting to nibble at a small patch of green. The dead man was in the middle of the road and the flies had gathered.

'Burgoyne?' Coop ventured.

'More than likely,' Thad agreed. 'Looks like Burgoyne got himself a fresh horse and heaven help Rowdy and that little girl!'

Rowdy saw that they weren't going to be able to outrun the rider and get to town before he caught them. The rider had them in sight and they couldn't hide. Neither could he stop and take a stand. There was no cover to be seen. Suddenly, he was terribly afraid for the girl and he hugged her closer to his chest.

Rowdy knew the rider was within rifle range but he wasn't firing. He didn't know that Burgoyne, in his haste and confusion from the heat and thirst, forgot that his rifle was in its holster on his exhausted horse. The unfortunate rider from whom he stole the horse had been unarmed. Burgoyne had to overtake them or get off a lucky shot with a pistol to stop the rescue.

Rowdy heard the first shot. He heard a second shot and he heard the slug sizzle by just over his head. He looked back. The rider would have him in only moments. Suddenly Rowdy felt a horrible burning pain in his left side over his ribs and he nearly fell out of the saddle. He knew he had been shot and he didn't know how long he would be conscious. He and Alma would be dead in seconds if he went straight on so he took a desperate measure.

Rowdy hauled back on the reins with everything he had and Traveller stumbled and came to a stop. Rowdy wheeled him around so his right side was facing the approaching gunman. He drew his pistol, thumbed back the hammer, and shielding Alma with his body, fired at the horseman about to ride them down.

CHAPTER 11

The galloping horse fell as if it had been guillotined. The rider smashed into the dirt of the road face first and cried out as the horse's flank fell on him. To get that quick kill, Rowdy knew that the big Henry .44 slug had hit the horse in the brain, killing it instantly.

Rowdy urged Traveller into a walk toward the downed rider. The man was still alive. He looked up and saw Rowdy and the girl a few feet away. His pistol lay on the road within arm's length and he reached for it.

'Don't,' Rowdy shouted. In a rage Burgoyne reached for the pistol, seized it and brought it up for one last shot.

Rowdy covered Alma's eyes with his left hand and shot Burgoyne through the head.

He was vaguely aware that people were shouting and someone was riding toward him from Amargosa. He heard Alma cry 'Tio Roy, Tio Roy,' and she jumped down from the saddle. She was safe and he was terribly tired. He could rest now.

Unconscious, he fell out of the saddle onto the Jericho Road.

After dark, two more riders came into town. They went directly to the sheriff's office and went in. Roy Fresquez was sitting in the sheriff's chair drinking coffee. He looked up at them and jumped to his feet, smiling broadly.

'Thank God,' he said. 'You're alive!'

'Did you expect anything else?' Thad said.

'I didn't know what to expect after Rowdy got here and the shape he was in,' the deputy said.

'What? Did something happen to Rowdy? Is he alive?' Thad asked, panicked.

'He's been shot, but Alma is safe, not a scratch,' Fresquez replied. 'Rowdy had a gun battle right at the edge of town with some bird that was chasing him. It turned out to be Burgoyne. Rowdy won, but he's in bad shape. He's at the doc's office. We can go over there if you want.'

'We want to,' Thad said.

'I took Alma back to her father and he's taken her and her mother and her brother to a safe place,' Fresquez added as they went out the door. 'Now the old man's ready to go to war,' he added with a broad smile. 'By the way, did you finish your business in Jericho?'

'The business is satisfactorily completed,' Coop said. 'Mr Isaac Cripps' future associates will be the worms.'

'Someday, you'll have to tell me the story,' the deputy said.

'Coop should be able to make a good story out of it,' Thad said. 'He had a unique view of the whole thing.'

At the doctor's office they looked in on a sleeping Rowdy. The doctor said he was sleeping from the opiate he had given him to ease the pain and make him sleep. The doctor added that his injury was serious and would have knocked an ordinary man down on his back. But somehow Rowdy not only survived the wound, he managed to kill his attacker before losing consciousness and falling from the saddle. The doctor added that he had lost a lot of blood so the prognosis was uncertain at best, but the bullet or its fragments did not touch the heart or the lungs so the doctor felt optimistic even though two ribs were badly damaged.

After making certain that all was being done for Rowdy that could be, Thad and Coop arranged boarding for their horses and Traveller, then checked into the hotel. Thad took off his boots and laid down on his bed and said, 'I'm plumb tuckered out.'

Coop said, 'Well my goodness, I wonder why. You didn't get any sleep last night, you killed a man this morning before breakfast, you rode a horse thirty miles in the blazing sun, then found out one of your closest friends damn near got killed. I don't know why you're tuckered out either.'

Thad didn't reply. He was already snoring.

The next morning, Thad and Coop visited Rowdy, who seemed to be coming around, and went to the sheriff's office to discuss plans for ridding the county of Comanche Holdings and its agents.

Sheriff Rogers, looking like a new man to Thad, greeted the young men and told them that their efforts in bringing his daughter back to her family were truly heroic. Thad assured him that Rowdy carried out the actual rescue while they themselves supplied the ruse to get the kidnapper out of the house. Mr Aldama, who had recruited the Apache Wells boys, was close to tears of joy.

After the compliments and congratulations were exhausted, they got down to business on how to deal with the thugs employed by Comanche Holdings. Sheriff Rogers had sat down with the county judge the night before working on warrants for the arrest of the Comanche Holdings people and a search warrant for the Comanche Holdings office that was in the next block. For some weeks, under Sheriff Rogers orders, Fresquez had been secretly obtaining statements from several witnesses to company crimes and one eyewitness to a murder. The deputy had kept the information secret to protect those witnesses. This information was evidence needed to obtain the warrants.

Fresquez had already advised the witnesses that their names would be used in such a manner today and each had made provision to be out of town or hiding at a friend's house. Before the thugs could track down any witness, the warrant would be served, company records would be seized and the guilty employees would be arrested. Timing was essential to safeguard everyone concerned.

The sheriff's plan was this: immediately after obtaining the warrant, Sheriff Rogers and Deputy Fresquez would go directly to the Comanche Holdings office and seize their records and place anyone in the office under arrest. Thad and Coop, officially deputized and armed with a warrant, would arrest Schwartz and Benet in their rooms at the hotel and bring them back to the gaol. They would then go to the home of a Dolly Morgan and take Strang into custody. The plan had to be carried out quickly before the alarm could be raised to prevent any of the gang from fleeing.

After everyone agreed on their assignments, Sheriff Rogers swore in Thad and Coop then left with Deputy Fresquez for the county judge's office. The sheriff had notified the judge the night before of what he would be asking. The judge, being a county landowner himself was enthusiastic.

When the sheriff returned with his warrants, Thad and Coop took their warrants and went directly to the hotel. They served a warrant on the manager who was manning the desk that morning. When he saw the names on the warrant, he paled visibly and asked to be let off the hook.

'Please understand,' he said. 'I am just a hotel manager. I know nothing of arresting people and firearms and violence and that sort of thing.'

Thad explained to him that all he had to do was unlock the doors and step back. He would be put in no mortal danger. After extended brow beating and assurances, he reluctantly accompanied the two new deputies, his knees shaking and his hands trembling, to the rooms of the accused. The key ring that contained the master key held multiple keys and the manager's hands were shaking so violently the key ring clinked like a bag of big coins.

Thad told him to remove the master key from the ring and give it to him. The manager did so then fled.

They went to room fourteen, Benet's room. Thad stood beside the door and carefully turned the key in the lock. He eased the door open on an empty room. Benet's bed was empty. Thad pulled the door closed and they went to room nine, Shwartz's room.

Thad slowly turned the key in the lock and eased the door open. Schwartz was sleeping heavily and heard nothing. They stepped into the room and Thad eased the door shut. Coop moved close to the bed looking down at Schwartz. Thad took up a position on the other side of the bed and pulled a set of manacles from his back pocket. Schwartz was sleeping on his right side. Thad nodded to Coop and clamped the manacles on the gunman's left wrist. Coop immediately pulled him over on his stomach and Thad grabbed his right arm and slapped the manacles over his right wrist before he was awake enough to know what was happening. Thad sat on his legs to fasten the leg irons but Schwartz started to cry out and Coop slammed the pillow over his face and held it down.

Schwartz kicked and cried out until Coop leaned close to the pillow and said, 'I'll take the pillow off your face but you yell or kick, I'll hit you with my gun butt.'

Schwartz was suddenly still. Coop removed the pillow and Schwartz grimaced and squinted his eyes at his two captors while Thad fastened the leg irons.

'What in hell do you want?' he demanded.

'Just you, old cowboy, just you,' Coop said. 'Get up on your feet. That chain will let you take steps of about a foot and a half.'

'Where are we going?' Schwartz asked.

'The hoosegow,' Coop said.

As they descended the stairs to the hotel lobby, Thad asked, 'Where is your frog friend, Benet?'

'How the hell should I know?' Schwartz snarled, 'He was chasing a piece of quim last time I saw 'im.'

'Oh well,' Coop said. 'We'll figure it out when we get to the gaol. Fresquez tells me they have an anvil and a hammer in back for interrogating prisoners, uses them for the toes.'

'Wait a minute!' Schwartz screamed. 'What's going on here? That sheriff can't do nothin' to us!'

'I'm afraid you're wrong,' Thad chuckled. 'His little girl was returned to him last night. Now she's in a safe place where you would-be child killers can't find her. And by the way, your friend Burgoyne got his brains blown out on the Jericho Road last night.'

'And this morning,' Coop added, 'the sheriff served a warrant on your company and seized all the company records.'

Schwartz paled as he realized that the Comanche Holdings Company scheme was unravelling.

'Now wait a minute, you fellows,' he squeaked. 'We can work something out here. There ain't no reason for everybody goin' to gaol. If you got Beale, you got who you need. I'm just a hired hand, I don't know nothin' 'bout the company.'

'You just follow orders, is that it?' Thad said.

'Sure,' Schwartz answered, a glimmer of hope in his eyes. 'We just do what we're told to do. I'm just an errand boy. You unnerstand that, don't cha?'

'I understand perfectly,' Thad said. 'That's why you are going to hang.'

Schwartz gulped and stared in horror at Thad.

'Where is Benet?' Coop asked.

Schwartz screamed, 'You dirty bastards, you sneaky coyote sons of bitches, I ain't telling you jack shit.'

Coop sighed and started explaining as if he were talking to a slow-witted child. 'The way the hammer and anvil works is, we put your foot on the top of the anvil and we play eenie, meenie, minie, moe and we pick a toe and hit it with the hammer. Then if you don't tell us what we need to know, we play again and smash another toe. Of course, we have to do it fast because those smashed toes tend to go bad and turn black and stink, and the doctor has to cut 'em off.'

Schwartz threw back his head and screamed.

Thad and Coop delivered Schwartz to the gaol where they briefly discussed Benet's where-abouts. Since Schwartz did not care to test his resolve and his loyalty to the company, he told Thad that Benet was at Dolly Morgan's house along with Strang. Benet was with a friend of Dolly's and the couple planned to spend the night at Dolly's house.

As they rode toward Dolly Morgan's house, Coop said, 'Rowdy is going to be disappointed that he missed all this.'

'I don't know,' Thad said with a trace of doubt. 'It's been Sunday-on-a-farm so far but getting those two out of that woman's house may be a different story.'

They saw the house at a distance. There was a horse shed and what looked like a tool shed in back of the house. Then they saw there was a horse tied up in front.

'Oh, oh,' Thad grunted. 'One horse?'

They both reined in their mounts. At the same time, there was a muzzle flash from a window of the house and a bullet sizzled by Thad's head. Thad drew his .44 and fired three quick rounds at the window and grabbed his carbine from the saddle holster as he and Coop jumped out of their saddles. They whacked their horses on their rumps to make them get clear and dove to the ground. The sniper fired again and kicked up dust and gravel by Coop's head. A rock stung his cheek. The two scrambled for a rock wall just off the road.

The shooter fired two more shots before they gained the shelter of the wall.

'You just had to say something, didn't you,' Coop asked Thad.

'I can say "I told you so",' Thad responded.

'Wonder who owns that horse?' Coop said to no one in particular.

'Someone we didn't know about, apparently,' Thad said. 'Whoever it is probably saw us hustling Schwartz across the street to the gaol and decided to help out his friends. Now what?'

Coop said, 'It's open ground between here and that house. There's no way we can rush them and waiting till dark is going to be all day.'

'Let's just hope Fresquez gets curious as to why we are not back and comes looking.' Thad grunted. 'It's going to get hot and thirsty out here.'

Thad rose up with his carbine and fired at the

window where he had seen the muzzle flash. A shot answered him and struck the wall, the flattened slug whining as it ricocheted.

'We can't get in there unless we go a long way around,' Thad mused, looking at the length of the wall. 'They can't get to us unless they sneak out the back and somehow manage to get to the wall down the way without our seeing them. I think I'll work my way down the wall to wherever it goes and get a look from there. There may be a way to come up on them from behind.'

'I'll just rest here in the sun while you do that,' Coop said. When Thad looked back at him, he grinned, he said, 'I'll fire a shot every once in a while just to keep 'em on their toes.'

Thad, sometimes in a crouch and sometimes running on all fours, travelled the length of the wall. It ran for some two hundred yards before coming to a corner with another wall and angling off to Thad's right. He rose up cautiously and glanced over the wall. Just twenty yards from the wall, there was a dry wash that offered cover. The house that sheltered Strang and Benet was at the top of a slope that began at the road. The ground dropped away gently from the house to Thad's present position. The start of the wash started perhaps thirty to forty yards in back of Dolly's place. He reasoned that if he could get to the wash, he would not be visible from the house until he was close to the outbuildings.

He heard Coop firing. He was over the wall and scrambling for the dry wash in an instant. He made it to the edge, scooted over and took a seven-foot slide to the bottom. He got up, drew his pistol and loaded the empty chambers. With his carbine at the ready, he moved cautiously and quietly along the wash, listening for any sign that he shared it with someone else. During the rare rain, the wash was fed from several places along its length. Those smaller washes provided cover for someone who might be waiting for someone to move into his sights. Thad moved along the uneven gully, sometimes fighting to stay upright when the dry mud beneath him crumpled. He reasoned that he had covered fifty to sixty yards when he heard a rustling noise somewhere ahead. It sounded as if a sizeable portion of the gully wall had given way. He went to the side of the wash and pressed himself into one of the feeder gullies and waited.

Soon, he heard movement along the wash. When the person came into sight, it was not Benet or Strang. It appeared to be a young cowhand, picking his way along the uncertain ground.

Thad raised his rifle and shouted, 'Don't move!'

The cowhand went for his pistol and Thad fired. The boy fell backward and screamed. Thad was upon him in an instant. He picked up the boy's pistol, stuck it in his belt and bent over the groaning boy to examine him. Thad was happy to see the wound was not immediately life threatening. He had hit the boy's arm. The bullet had gone on to hit the boy along the side of his waist, but only furrowed the skin and did not penetrate the body.

'Where you the one that warned them?' Thad demanded.

'Yes.' The boy said. 'Am I going to die?'

'Not yet, son,' Thad answered. 'Did they send you out here to get behind us?'

'Yessir,' the boy replied, gasping from the pain.

'You hold on and don't make any noise. I'll settle up with those two inside and I'll get a doctor for you.'

'Please, mister. Don't let me die,' the boy said.

'I won't.'

Thad made his way to the origin of the wash, not far behind Dolly's outbuildings. He peered cautiously over the edge, climbed out and ran to the back of the horse shed. He started to peer around the corner of the building when a fusillade of shots broke out. He ducked back instinctively then realized the shots were not directed at him. He looked around the corner and could

151

see the end of the stone wall where he had left Coop. But there was not one pistol firing over the wall, there were three rifles! Sheriff Rogers and Fresquez had joined Coop in the attack on the house.

Thad moved around to where he had an unobstructed view of the house's back door and waited. The gun battle kept on, but it was decidedly uneven. The firing continued without let up. Suddenly the back door burst open and Strang and Benet ran full tilt toward the horse shed. They were trying to get their horses and escape!

Thad stepped around the corner into full view and shouted, 'Hold it and get your hands up.'

Strang went for his pistol and Thad shot him in the chest. Strang's legs buckled and his inertia carried him forward on his face. As Strang was falling, Thad levered another round into the breech and went to kill Benet but his target threw down his pistol and fell to his knees with his hands up yelling, 'Don't shoot, don't shoot!'

CHAPTER 12

They got the wounded boy back into town and under the doctor's care. They learned that the boy, who had no home, had been promised employment by Beale's people and therefore took their side. Coop had a cut on his face caused by a fragment of stone knocked off the stone wall by a bullet. The doctor treated it with a dash of iodine.

Fresquez and the sheriff had arrested Beale and his bookkeeper and gaoled them, then went to check on Thad and Coop. They found Coop alone, firing away with a pistol with a hot barrel. They had brought rifles 'just in case' and joined the fight.

Sheriff Rogers was almost euphoric. His daughter was safe, the killers were dead or in gaol and Beale, the headman, occupied his very own cell in the county's accommodations. The sheriff explained to Thad that it would take some time to sort out what the holding company had done and return the property to the rightful heirs of the murdered men, but the judge was eager to get started.

Sheriff Rogers took Thad and Coop aside to talk to them about Rowdy.

'I have talked to Rowdy about a job working with me as deputy sheriff after he recovers. I understand he has no people back in Apache Wells, or anywhere else, for that matter. He said he would miss you fellows something terrible but he figured he was going to have to settle down sometime anyway. I just wanted to give you a little warning before you talked to him. I don't know when I seen a man stronger or with more grit in his craw than that big fellow.'

After a small celebration during which everyone bragged on the boys from Apache Wells until it got embarrassing, Thad and Coop visited Rowdy. He was waiting to hear what happened with those 'smart-alecs' that tried to intimidate them that day downtown on the boardwalk. Coop and Thad related the story of the gunfight in Jericho and the shootout in which Strang died and Benet surrendered.

When the laughter tapered off, Rowdy became serious. 'I suppose the sheriff has told you about him offerin' me a job as a deputy?'

'Yes, he has,' Thad said while Coop nodded.

'Well,' Rowdy went on, 'you remember we talked about settlin' down and getting responsible jobs? When the sheriff asked me, I said to myself, Rowdy, this is a sign. You better take the job. You ain't a kid any more and besides, that Thad Forrester has been gettin' you into some tight spots lately.'

When he stopped laughing, Thad said, 'Rowdy, I always thought you'd be the last one of us that decided to grow up and danged if you aren't the first! I've got to tell both of you that I'm going to take the same road. This trip could have turned out a disaster for all of us. Coop, if I had any idea I was going to put you in that fix with a cocked six-gun pointing at your head, I never would have left Apache Wells. I would have just said to hell with Isaac Cripps and have done with it. But I wanted to get even with Cripps so damned bad. I wasn't thinking of anything except how bad I hated him; someone I had never met. Because I didn't know how bad people can really be, I could have gotten both of you killed. What's the point of getting even when you lose someone you really care about?'

'But you have to consider, Thad,' Coop said. 'We three are each five hundred dollars richer, Rowdy has a job, Alma is back with her family and some very bad people are dead or in gaol. I think it turned out pretty darned well.'

Thad and Coop were giving Rowdy an emotional goodbye when Aldama joined them.

'Young gentlemen,' he said. 'I have with me the fees that we of the citizens committee promised for your help in ridding us of those monsters. It is small reward considering the risks you took and the injury that *Señor* Rowdy is now enduring. Let this money be a symbol of our heartfelt thanks and eternal gratitude.'

Aldama's speech and the money had the effect of lifting their spirits and interrupting what might have been an overly emotional good-bye. Thad and Coop promised faithfully to visit the first chance they got, wishing Rowdy well in his new job.

Coop said, 'The next time we see you, you may have a couple of little cowboys hanging on to you if that tall gal down town has her way.'

Rowdy said, 'If you come to visit, let me know ahead of time so I can meet you on the other side of Yucca. I'll tell them Yuccans that y'all are my prisoners and they can't have you.'

It took a while for Thad and Coop to make the trip back to Apache Wells. They had to make a wide detour around Yucca because they knew they would be shot, or at least gaoled, on sight. At Cruz, they went into town quietly and left early the next morning, rather than take a chance on meeting the town marshal who did not welcome killers into his town. Coop left a note with the blacksmith to be delivered to the marshal, telling him that he had one less demon to wrestle because Isaac Cripps had gone to meet his maker.

They had camped for the last time and were on the last leg of the trip when Coop spoke.

'You're going back and marry Lila Beth and get a job, right?'

'That's my plan,' Thad said. 'Do you have one?'

'Yep, I do,' Coop said. 'I got to grind the rough corners off it but I've got one.'

'What is it?'

'I've got five hundred dollars. I can live a while on that. I think I'm going to mosey over to San Antonio and see if I can't get into some college.'

'College?' Thad said. He stopped his horse in the road. 'College?' he repeated. He thought for a while and finally said, 'Well, I suppose that does make sense. What are you going to study?'

'I don't know, but I know it sure as hell won't involve hunting for outlaws.'

As they came within sight of Apache Wells, Thad's pulse quickened and excitement butter-flied in his stomach. Somehow, the town looked a bit different to him. He wondered why and realized maybe it wasn't the town, but probably his eyes that made it look different.

When they reached the main street, people who had given them up for dead recognized them, smiled and waved or hollered a welcome. As other people noticed they began to shout and whistle. The boys saw Daureen come out of her café to watch them.

'Where' the big one?' she hollered.

'He's back in Amargosa and he's got a girl friend,' Thad answered.

'Did you get your man?' she asked.

'Got him and a little extra,' Thad answered.

The sheriff heard the exchange and he came out of his office and his mouth fell open. He leaned against a post and took a deep breath then wiped at his eyes with a handkerchief. Someone ran into Flower's legal office to tell Lila and she came out on the boardwalk with her hands on her hips. Thad saw her and felt his heart swell in his chest until he wanted to sob.

He rode to the boardwalk in front of the office and jumped down from the saddle and Coop reined to a stop.

'Where's Rowdy,' she asked, concern in her eyes.

'He's fine,' Thad replied. 'He's a hero and he's already got a steady job.'

'How about you? Are you home for good?' she asked. 'Is that man dead?'

He took Lila in his arms and kissed her like

there was no one else around, ignoring the whoops and the whistles. He looked in her eyes and said, 'You don't ever have to think about that man again. I'm home for good. What I had to do is done. I know what I want and it's not anything like riding that road to Jericho. It's living here with you and making a home, one like my folks had.'

He took her in his arms again.

Coop watched for a while then he leaned over and whispered into Othello's ear. 'Well, old boy, we'll have to see how things end up for us, but for right here and now, it looks like a happy ending . . . or a heck of a start.'